She Could Ever Have...

wouldn't it be worth it?

"I feel as if I've waited all my life for you," Cul said. "Every woman I've touched in the past six years has been you."

That admission brought tears to Bett's eyes. He meant it; it was in every line of his face. And if he wanted her that much, couldn't it mean that he cared, just a little?

As the passion left her mind, it became sharp again, and she remembered the pain of being pushed aside. She wondered if she was strong enough to go through it again.

"Bett," he said gently. "Don't brood about it. Tonight we'll talk. We'll make plans."

"What kind of plans are there to make?" she asked sadly. "You'll take me to bed, and I'll let you, and in the morning you'll be gone."

"No," Cul said. "I'm no stronger than you are. If we make love, it won't just be a one-night stand. You're my woman. Tonight I'll even prove it to you."

Dear Reader,

Welcome to Silhouette! Our goal is to give you hours of unbeatable reading pleasure, and we hope you'll enjoy each month's six new Silhouette Desires. These sensual, provocative love stories are both believable and compelling—sometimes they're poignant, sometimes humorous, but always enjoyable.

Indulge yourself. Experience all the passion and excitement of falling in love along with our heroine as she meets the irresistible man of her dreams and together they overcome all obstacles in the path to a happy ending.

If this is your first Desire, I hope it'll be the first of many. If you're already a Silhouette Desire reader, thanks for your support! Look for some of your favorite authors in the coming months: Stephanie James, Diana Palmer, Dixie Browning, Ann Major and Doreen Owens Malek, to name just a few.

Happy reading!

Isabel Swift
Senior Editor

SDRL-7/85

DIANA PALMER
Loveplay

Silhouette Desire

Published by Silhouette Books New York
America's Publisher of Contemporary Romance

SILHOUETTE BOOKS
300 East 42nd St., New York, N.Y. 10017

ISBN: 0-373-05289-8

First Silhouette Books printing July 1986

Books by Diana Palmer

Silhouette Romance

Darling Enemy #254
Roomful of Roses #301
Heart of Ice #314
Passion Flower #328
Soldier of Fortune #340
After the Music #406
Champagne Girl #436

Silhouette Special Edition

Heather's Song #33
The Australian #239

Silhouette Desire

The Cowboy and the Lady #12
September Morning #26
Friends and Lovers #50
Fire and Ice #80
Snow Kisses #102
Diamond Girl #110
The Rawhide Man #157
Lady Love #175
Cattleman's Choice #193
The Tender Stranger #230
Love by Proxy #252
Eye of the Tiger #271
Loveplay #289

DIANA PALMER

is a prolific romance writer who got her start as a newspaper reporter. Accustomed to the daily deadlines of a journalist, she has no problem with writer's block. In fact, she averages a book every two months. The mother of a young son, Diana met and married her husband within one week: "It was just like something from one of my books."

To J.A.

One

The silence was eerie. Overhead, a single light burned in compliance with union rules. On the bare, quiet stage Bett Cambridge stood with a script in her slender hands and peered out into the darkened theater. The auditors were out there, she knew, but she couldn't see them. She'd been picked, one of three girls out of an open call. She'd read for those unknown auditors once before, material from the same play she was reading for again on the callback. The fear was worse this time. They had to be interested, or why would they have asked her to come back?

She knew the play well, she knew the role she was trying for. It was as familiar as her own name, because it had been so much a part of its author. She shouldn't have come here. What if he showed up? But she needed the part so badly, and, after all, it was a revival of the old play. Wasn't he in Hollywood, working on a screenplay? The slender hands holding the script trembled just a little. It would be all right.

Anyway, it wasn't as if there was still anything between them. Edward McCullough was well and truly out of her league these days, what with his celebrated reputation as a playwright. Cul wouldn't care. He'd put Bett Cambridge right out of his mind years ago, and he was keeping her out of it; his indifference told her so. Fleeting glimpses and infrequent conversations at parties were all the contact they had now. The past was dead and buried for both of them. So why should he mind her trying out for the revival of his hit play?

Her fingers clutched the script tightly as she let herself drift into the motivations of the part she was auditioning for. She would be playing a young girl, poor and alone and just under three months' pregnant. She'd dressed for the part the same as she had last time. She'd deliberately worn a shapeless corduroy jumper and let her long red-gold hair tangle around her shoulders. Now she slumped a little to simulate weariness. She thought of the sadness the poor and deserted girl would feel, and the sense of hopelessness. And then she began to read from Edward McCullough's *Girl in a Dark Room*.

"You'd have thought he was a gentleman, my Tom," she said in a clear tone that carried through the theater. She tossed back her hair and laughed. "You'd have thought he'd never have left me in the lurch. Good, kind Tom, who used to walk me home from the sewing plant every afternoon so's I wouldn't get

mugged. My Tom." She chewed on her lower lip and
closed her eyes, feeling the agony. "Oh, God, what's
to become of this baby inside me now? How can I have
it? How can I raise it? I got nobody, Lord! Not a
mama to help me fetch and carry, not a papa to scold
me. I got nobody on the face of this earth who gives a
damn if I live or die!" She put her face in her hands
and moved restlessly under the glare of the overhead
light. She lifted her head again and sighed, holding out
her hands in a gesture of futility. "I can't let somebody cut it out. I can't kill it. But I can't have it, neither, Lord. Oh, show me what to do!" she pleaded
half hoarsely, staring up into the darkness. She closed
her eyes and felt tears, real tears, start out of her eyes.
"Oh, God, please, if you love me, show me what to
do!"

She took a deep, slow breath, coming out of the
trance she'd put herself in. The dark auditorium came
back into focus. There was a long silence, then a muttered conversation. Bett stared out into the darkness,
waiting for the customary "Thank you" that would
tell her it was all over, and she hadn't got the part.
Please, she prayed silently, let me get the part.

A man rose from his dim seat and moved out into
the aisle. A tall man, powerfully built, with blond hair
that shone like new gold in sunlight. A man from out
of Bett's past, out of a nightmare. She hadn't expected
this. For God's sake, what was he doing here?

Edward McCullough came up onto the stage, looking as cynical as he always did when she rubbed him
the wrong way. He hadn't changed very much from
the days when he'd been a struggling actor and writing had only been some vague dream in his life. Now

he was one of the country's foremost playwrights, and looked it, in his white cashmere sweater and expensive tailored brown slacks. Older, and perhaps more worn. But he had something to show for it.

His chin lifted as he stopped just in front of Bett, and she lifted her own chin defiantly. Let him do his worst. She'd find another part—New York was a big city. She'd—

"Here we go again," he murmured, staring down into her rebellious dark eyes in her faintly freckled face. "Elisabet Cambridge, how you've changed since Atlanta."

She coolly lifted an eyebrow. She didn't smile—the girl who'd once loved him would have. Uninhibitedly, she'd have thrown herself wildly into his arms and invited him to take whatever he wanted. But Bett was older. And the only thing he possessed that she might have wanted now was a part in his play. Nothing more. Her eyes told him that, and more.

He laughed mockingly. "You haven't forgiven me, have you?" he asked. "What makes you think I'll give you this part, Bett?"

"Why should I tell you?" she asked. "I'll talk to the director about it."

"I *am* the director," Cul replied, his eyes gleaming at her obvious surprise. "Now, again," he continued softly, dangerously, "suppose you tell me what makes you think I'll give you this part?"

"Because I'm right for it," she said with quiet dignity. "Because I've played it so many times that I could do it blindfolded."

He looked down her slender body, letting his eyes rest contemplatively at her waist. "That may be so. But why should I give you the part, Bett?"

Bett swallowed. He wasn't going to make her back down. He knew, as she did, that she was perfect for the role. She didn't even have to put on a Southern accent; she already had one, left over from her childhood in Atlanta.

"Come on," he said curtly, "give me a reason."

"Because I'm in hock up to my ears," she said, her eyes glinting.

One eyebrow rose. "Not from what I've heard about you. You've had one successful run after another for the past two years. You were nominated for a Tony last year."

"And I enjoyed every penny," she agreed miserably. "Until my business manager talked me into investing heavily in what was supposed to be a riskless venture. I lost everything. All my savings are gone. Now I'm in debt, way over my head."

"So," he said heavily.

She shrugged. "Easy come, easy go?"

The phrase was one they'd exchanged all those years ago in Altanta when they were doing summer stock, and it brought back more memories than she'd expected it to. Her eyes lifted to his and he searched them coldly.

"Don't offer me the past, Elisabet," he said levelly. "I want no part of it, or you. Having a lovesick teenager hanging on my sleeve is something I can do without these days."

It took every ounce of willpower she had not to slap him. But she needed the part desperately, and he knew it. The mocking smile told her so.

He let her stew for a full minute before he said, carelessly, "You have the part, if you want it. Ted and James think you play the role magnificently, complete with accent."

"What do you think? You wrote it."

His slitted green eyes ran over her like hands. "You'll be adequate," he said flatly, and turned away.

"Adequate," Bett fumed when she went back to the apartment she shared with Janet Simms, a successful model. "Adequate! He never believed in me, never! He said I'd fall flat on my face six years ago. But I didn't," she added hotly. "I didn't! I came to New York, and I worked hard, and I've made a name for myself! I have a leather coat and an uptown apartment and a great future according to the reviewers...."

"And you owe the government your arms, legs and a year's salary," Janet reminded her, and sighed. "You crazy idiot, why did you have to try out for Cul's play?"

"Because I needed a job, and that was the only role going that I wanted to play," she said curtly. She sat down near the window, her face pensive. "Besides," she added, staring down into her lap. "Besides..."

"It was a glowing opportunity to get your knife into Edward McCullough?" Janet suggested. "At point-blank range?"

Bett shook her head wearily. "No. It's just that I couldn't resist the part. It has such feeling, such dramatic beauty..." She tangled her hands in her red-gold hair. "They hadn't announced the director. How could I have possibly known that Cul would turn up at the audition, for God's sake?"

"He's the playwright, too, why shouldn't he? Didn't you say he always has casting approval written into his contracts?"

"Yes," Bett said miserably. She stared at her feet, hating the size of them. She was tall and tended to be too slender, but at least she carried it gracefully.

"What are you going to do about the taxes?" Janet asked.

Bett shrugged. "I don't know." She looked up. "I've only thirty days to get up the estimated amount, from what my accountant told me. I'll have to cut corners like mad. And that means I can't stay here." She sighed miserably. In the past few days, her secure life had come tumbling around her ears. She was going to miss Janet terribly, but she couldn't possibly pay even half of the rent for the Park Avenue apartment. "I guess I'll work everything out somehow."

"Of course you will," Janet said bracingly. "After all, you talked the director of that nude play about Elizabeth the First into letting you wear a corset."

"Remind me to tell you all about that someday." Bett chuckled. "I always seem to get picked for Elizabeth."

"You look exactly like paintings of her," Janet said. "Except that your hairline isn't as far back, and your skin isn't as white. But the eyes, and the facial features, even the color of your hair is so like hers..." She grinned. "And she was a virgin, too."

"Don't say that out loud, somebody might hear you!" Bett exclaimed, laughing. "I'm supposed to be three months' pregnant in the play!"

"A biological first—pregnancy without fertilization. Just think, it will make all the medical journals," Janet teased.

"Want to go apartment hunting with me?" Bett asked as she got her coat and headed for the door.

"I guess I'd better. I do know the turf better than you do. Just let me get a coat."

Bett wished she hadn't had to sell her pretty leather one. With a sigh, she examined her threadworn coat, an old tweed one that she kept for sentimental reasons. Cul had taken her walking through Piedmont Park one late spring day, and she'd worn that coat....

Her eyes clouded. She slipped on the tweed without any real enthusiasm and followed Janet out the door.

The apartment they found was a shocking change from her former quarters. It was in Queens, on the top floor of a tenement building, and the noise from her neighbors was nonstop.

"I can't leave you here," Janet said firmly. "I can't. Come with me, we'll find something else."

"No. It's perfect," Bett said, glancing around at the white dinette set with the peeling paint, the counter with its broken Formica top and the living room with its swaybacked sofa and matching chair with torn fabric.

"The health department would condemn it even after it was cleaned up," Janet protested.

"Just right for a struggling actress," Bett said with a forced smile. "After all, I started out in a place like this. First I'll take care of the rent, and then we'll go out and stock this place with a few groceries."

"We can get you some curtains, too," Janet added thoughtfully. "And maybe a throw cover for that awful sofa, and a couple of bushy plants—"

"We can not," Bett interrupted her. "I don't have the luxury of living up to my celebrity status anymore. Remember, I'm going to be on a tight budget for a long time."

Janet only moaned, muttering something about the fickleness of fate.

Two

It was like old times for Bett, who'd lived like this in her younger days. She still knew where to go for bargains and what to buy. And the fact that it was New York and not Atlanta didn't make a bit of difference. Poverty had many addresses.

"I don't understand why you won't just let me pay the rent until you get out of the hole," Jane said later as she helped Bett move the few things she had to have into her new home.

"Because I'll be working for minimum wage through all six weeks of rehearsals," she told her friend. "And then we'll have a tryout in Philadelphia before we open on Broadway. I don't know when I'll be able to make a decent living. And I don't want to owe anybody, Janet. Not even you," she added with a quiet smile. She sat down on the lumpy sofa with a sigh. "Once I start earning, and pay back what I owe the IRS, I'll come home."

"Okay. I guess you know best." Janet watched her friend stack dishes on the counter. "But it's going to be lonely without you."

"You can come over for supper tomorrow night. I'll make spaghetti."

"That sounds nice. You can come for supper the night after, and move back in."

Bett laughed softly. "I'll miss you, too. But it will all work out."

"Sure."

"Really!"

Janet smiled. "Okay. I'll try to adopt an optimistic attitude. Now, tell me what you want me to help with. I don't have anything to do for the rest of the day, fortunately for you."

"You're not kidding. I never realized I had so much stuff to move!"

It took the rest of the day to get only half the things in their proper place. By the time Janet left, Bett was too tired to do anything except go to bed.

Her dreams were restless and unnerving and full of Cul. She woke up before dawn to the sound of a screaming child in the apartment above and couldn't close her eyes again. She got up and made coffee, and stared out the window at the wall across the way. The only view was straight up, and it was too chilly to lean that far out the window.

She sipped her coffee, remembering how it had been six years ago. She had been a struggling young actress then, and Cul had written his first play. It was being

performed by the local summer stock theater where the
two of them had been performing for several weeks.
Up until that time, she and Edward McCullough had
been moderately friendly—it was impossible to work
in such a small group of people without getting to
know each of them. But Bett had been much more involved emotionally than Cul, from the very beginning. She remembered looking at him when he was
introduced as the group's newest player, and wanting
him with a wild fever. Considering her puritanical
upbringing in Atlanta, and her virginal status, it was
surprising to find a man having that effect on her.

Because he bothered her so much physically, she'd
begun needling him. It was a habit that took hold
early, and had a lasting effect. Cul took it with unexpected good humor. And then they began rehearsals
on his new play.

Bett, because of her unusual coloring and talent,
had been given the female lead. Cul would have been
perfect for the male lead, but had refused it, giving the
part instead to Charles Tanner, an actor of large pro-
portions and moderate talent.

The female part was that of a liberated young
woman out on her own and enjoying liaisons. The
male part was frankly reticent and condemning. The
play contrasted the conservative viewpoint with the
liberated one, and did such a splendid job of it that
Cul was approached by a theatrical backer. Shortly
thereafter he left for New York. But not before he'd
done some devastating damage to Bett's emotions.

She'd always told herself that she had followed him
to New York because of his cold observation that
she'd never be star material with all her hang-ups. But

sometimes she wondered if it wasn't because she'd loved him so much.

Her eyes closed and she could see them together that first evening, when he'd been coaching her in the part.

"You just can't let go, can you, Bett?" he'd accused coldly after a half-dozen failed attempts at dialogue. He'd slammed the script down on the coffee table in his small apartment and reached for her. "Well, baby, let's see if this kind of coaching isn't what you need the most . . . !" And he'd kissed her.

Six years later, she could still feel the wild impact of his mouth on hers. Months of watching him, hoping, praying for just a few seconds in his arms, and it had happened just that suddenly.

She remembered going stiff from the burst of pleasure, mingled with apprehension, at the intimacy of his hold. Cul was eight years her senior and obviously experienced, and she hadn't known what he'd expected from her. The expression on his face when he lifted his head had been a revelation.

"Is that the best you can do?" he'd asked wonderingly.

She'd flushed and tried to get away, but he'd held her securely against his long, lean body. There was steel in his fingers, in the wiry arms that held her.

"Not yet," he'd murmured, studying her. "You've always reminded me of Elizabeth the First. Do you remember what they called her, Bett?"

She'd chewed on her full lower lip to stay its trembling. "Yes."

"The Virgin Queen," he'd continued quietly, searching her face. "Do you have that in common with her, too, as well as her hair and eyes?"

She'd tried to avert her eyes, but he'd held her face up to his intense study.

"No wonder you can't play the part properly," he'd said then. And he'd smiled. "All right, Miss Hang-ups. Let's see what we can do about those unexpected inhibitions."

And he'd kissed her again. This time it had been give and take, advance and retreat, until he woke the sleeping fires in her and she arched up and gave him her heart.

He'd sent her home minutes later, without taking what she'd been so eager to give him. And for the weeks that followed, they'd been inseparable, on stage and off. By the end of the summer, she'd been totally committed, and hoping for happily ever after.

It had come as a wild shock when Cul broke it off. Abruptly, without warning, announcing in front of the entire company, including Bett, that he was leaving for New York to direct his play on Broadway.

Bett had gone to his apartment that evening to wait for him. And he'd come home with one of the women in the cast, one with a reputation for giving out, and he'd laughed at Bett's quiet query about the future of their relationship. Both of them had laughed. And Bett had cried herself to sleep. But it had gotten worse. The next day, the whole cast knew about it. Cul left and Bett gritted her teeth and tried to play out the season. But his parting shot had been that she was limited to small summer stock groups, and she'd de-termined immediately to show him she wasn't. She'd gotten on the next plane to New York, and there she'd been ever since.

She sipped her cold coffee with downcast eyes. Well, he'd told her from the very beginning that he wouldn't get involved with her physically. He wouldn't take her virginity, even though she blatantly offered it. Perhaps it was as well. He'd announced loudly, and to anyone who cared to listen, that marriage wasn't one of his future goals. He planned to go through life single, and despite the fact that he and Bett had been a brief item, it was a relationship without a future.

But they'd had a special kind of relationship, for all that. She could talk to him as she could talk to no one else. And he seemed to confide in her, as much as he confided in anyone. There were still unexplored depths to his character that she doubted anyone had ever plumbed. He was a zealously private person.

When she came to New York, it was inevitable that as she started to climb up from part to part, they'd meet socially. She still occasionally needled him in the old way, and he took it all with unexpected good humor. She wondered if sometimes he didn't see through the playing to the deep hurt he'd inflicted, and tolerated her biting remarks for that reason.

But the thirst for revenge was still strong, and flared up every so often. He'd never know how bitterly he'd hurt her, how he'd damaged her budding emotions. She hadn't been capable of a deep relationship since the day he walked out. Perhaps she never would be. And for that, she owed him.

She poured out the rest of the coffee and went to get dressed.

The first day of rehearsal was exciting. She liked the rest of the cast immediately. The play promised to be great, and everyone hoped it would have a long run on

Broadway. Considering what it cost to produce, it would be a disaster if it folded too soon. Of course, any play was a risk. But with the caliber of Cul's script, and its previous long run many years before, they felt it couldn't help but hit.

Cul spoke to the players, lingering on the good fortune of finding an actress with Bett's talent. For the first day, since he was doubling as director, he worked out the blocking —the deft art of moving actors and actresses around the stage without having them run over each other while they spoke their lines. Each movement had to have motivation, and since the actors were working from scripts, not memorized dialogue, it was more difficult. Bett knew from the old days that, by the third day, Cul would expect them to do the entire play without the scripts.

Bett obeyed quickly and without argument as Cul gave her directions, and she went carefully through her own blocking, noting it on her script.

But the actor who was playing opposite her, a method actor who came from a well-known acting school in the city, had to have his motivation for each step spelled out. Cul obliged with unexpected patience, explaining as they went along. Unfortunately the actor disagreed with half the moves and wanted to rearrange his own movements. The resulting exchange of viewpoints went on for a half hour, until Cul politely told the man to either do it as he was told or find another play.

"Now, Cul," David Hadison said soothingly, "you know there isn't a better play in town. I gave up a movie contract to play this for you. Doesn't that entitle me to one tiny change?"

David was tall and dark, and inclined to moods, but he was a splendid actor. Cul sighed and gave in, but only on one short walk across the stage. That seemed to satisfy David, though, because he didn't put up any more argument. He spent the rest of the long, arduous rehearsal grinning at Bett.

She carried her script home and studied it until her eyes blurred, practicing loudly despite the wails of the baby upstairs and the off-key singing of the man below. There was so little time to learn the dialogue. Most of it was hers, not David's, and she was meticulous over her lines. It was probably one of the reasons that Cul had given her the part.

The next morning she had most of it memorized, but the blocking tripped her up. She had to change a movement from center stage to stage left, around a table instead of in front of it, and it threw her rhythm off. She fumbled her lines, and Cul gave her a hard stare.

"I'm sorry," she murmured, "I blew it."

David grinned at her. "No problem. We all blow it from time to time. Even Cul used to, in the old days when he was one of the flock, didn't you, Cul?"

Cul only stared at him. "Let's take a ten minute break, kids," he said heavily, "and we'll get back to it. Bett, come here."

When he said it like that, it meant trouble. She followed him offstage without hesitant steps, remembering other conferences. She felt small in her jeans and sweatshirt as she followed his long strides backstage.

He fixed two cups of coffee and handed her one. "Now," he said. "What's wrong?"

"The blocking," she muttered. "You moved me in front of the table and it doesn't feel comfortable."

"If you go behind it, you'll upstage David."

"Yes, I know. I'm not complaining, it's just going to take me a day to get used to it, all right?" she asked defensively.

He sipped his coffee and glanced at her curiously, letting his eyes wander over her slimness, the long waves of her hair. "Do you play Elizabeth much these days?" he asked unexpectedly.

She smiled into her coffee. "Constantly," she muttered. "I'm typed, I suppose."

"In every way?" he probed.

She sipped the hot black liquid. "I didn't expect that you'd direct this revival," she said, sidestepping the question. "I thought you were in Hollywood working on a screenplay."

"I was. I asked if I could go to my apartment to work on it, and they said, sure." He chuckled. "I didn't mention that my apartment was in New York."

"William Faulkner once pulled that same trick, if I remember," she returned.

"A writer after my own heart. He was one of the greats." He leaned back against the wall with a sigh. "Why did you audition for my play, Bett?" he asked bluntly.

She looked up at him contemplatively, studying the new lines in his face, the dark tan that made his green eyes glitter like rain-washed leaves. "I needed the money."

"No," he replied. "That isn't what I meant. There are other plays in town."

She sighed and smiled wistfully. "There wasn't a role I had a better chance of getting," she admitted. "I know this one like the back of my hand. I didn't have time to wait for callbacks. I have thirty days to make a start on a very large tax bill. I can do it, but I have to live while I'm earning the rest of what I owe." She shrugged. "I didn't really think you'd be here, and I had this wild idea that I might get the part if I seemed polished enough." She glanced at him. "I played the role during that summer in Atlanta."

"Yes, I remember," he said curtly. He drank down the rest of his coffee. "Let's get back to it."

She would like to have pursued that line, to ask him why he'd broken it off so cruelly. But it was something that had happened a long time ago, and had no bearing on the present. She was an actress in need of money, and Cul was just the director. All too soon his part in the play would be over, and the stage manager, Dick Hamilton, would be in full charge of it all. Just a few weeks more to see Cul every day and agonize over the past. She started back toward the stage. Well, she'd live through it. She'd lived through six years without Cul, and this surely wasn't going to be that bad.

By the third day, the play was set, the blocking was done, and they were working without scripts. That was hard going on one or two of the players, but Bett didn't even notice. She had her lines down pat. It was just a matter of getting the right interpretation into them. Cul seemed to find fault with every sentence she uttered, despite the fact that she was doing it from memory, from coaching he'd given her during the short summer run in Atlanta.

By the end of the rehearsal late that night, she felt
dragged out and exhausted. She'd gotten out of the
habit of long hours, being between plays, and it was
rough adjusting to a day that ran from ten in the
morning until after eight or nine o'clock at night. Her
nerves were raw from Cul's criticism, and all she
wanted to do was crawl into bed.

But Cul stopped her at the stage door. "Not yet,
you don't," he said coolly. "Let's talk."

She felt like crying. She was so tired! "Cul. . ." she
began defensively, her eyes wistfully following the last
of the cast as they filed out the door and it closed behind them.

"You wanted this part," he reminded her with a
frankly cruel smile.

She glared at him through the glitter of tears. "Stupid me," she ground out. "I should have let them put
me in jail instead!"

"Save the emotion for your part. You're going to
need it." He turned away, leaving her to follow, and
picked up his script from one of the prop tables. He
threw himself down into a chair and crossed his long,
powerful legs. He ran his hand restlessly through his
already disheveled hair. "All right," he said gruffly.
"It starts breaking down here, on page thirty-six,
where you're explaining your pregnancy to David."

"Cul, I'm doing it the way you wanted it done in
Atlanta," she began.

His green eyes flashed angrily. "This isn't Atlanta.
And I've told you for the last time that I won't have
old ashes dredged up!"

"God forbid!" she agreed with a wild toss of her red-gold hair, her eyes flashing darkly. "I'm a little more choosy these days myself!"

He slammed the script onto the floor and stood up, towering over her. "You haven't changed," he said under his breath. "Not one bit. You're still the same undisciplined, impulsive, maddening little brat you used to be. But while you're starring in my damned play, you'll follow my direction, is that clear?"

Her pride felt as if he'd ripped it open. By her sides, her slender, graceful hands clenched until they hurt. "Yes, sir," she said in a hushed whisper.

His eyes studied her face quietly. "You've got more than your share of pride, haven't you? And much more than your share of temper. You always were passionate."

He couldn't have chosen a better way to hurt, and this time she couldn't stop it from showing. Her eyes closed and tears ran helplessly down her cheeks, although she didn't make a sound.

"Bett..." he ground out.

She turned away, dabbing at her eyes. "I'm very tired, Cul," she said with the last fragments of pride she could find. "Please, let's get on with it."

He hesitated for a long moment before he picked up the script and sat back down. When she took off her coat and turned, her face was composed, but very pale. He didn't miss that. His eyes narrowed as if it bothered him.

"I'm sorry," she said unexpectedly. "I should have gotten a job waiting on tables or something. I'm sorry I came here."

"So am I," he said curtly, "but it's too late to do anything about it now. I can't afford to lose any more time. As for the way you're playing the part, it's been six years. Will you try to remember that my outlook has changed, that my interpretations of the play have changed, and work with me instead of against me?"

She sighed wearily. "Yes."

"Then, let's start from your first line on page thirty-six," he said, leaning back.

She ran through it again, remembering the way he'd coached her earlier, and he nodded as he listened, his lips pursed, his eyes narrowed as he took in even her body movements.

"Much better," he said when she finished. "Much better. You understand now, don't you, that I want as much emotion as you can drag up. I want the audience to cry buckets when you give that monologue about not giving up the baby."

"I understand." She pulled her coat back on, lifting her long hair out of the way. "You never used to like so much emotion in the monologue."

"I'm older."

"So am I," she said quietly. She picked up her own script and tucked it under her arm along with her purse. "You do a lot of plays about pregnancy these days," she observed. "And yet you've never married. Don't you want—"

"It's late," he said shortly, checking his watch, "and I have a late date. I'll drop you off by your apartment."

"No!" she said quickly, for some reason not wanting him to see where she lived. "I'll get a cab."

He scowled, but he didn't pursue it. "Suit yourself, darling."

If he'd known how that careless endearment hurt, she thought miserably, he'd probably have used it ten times as much. Once he'd used it and meant it, so long ago.

He hailed a cab and put her into it, turning away immediately, and she forced herself not to watch him walk away. Minutes later she was back at her apartment and in her bed. She fell asleep the minute her head touched the pillow.

Bett slept badly, and dragged into rehearsal a half hour early with a cup of black coffee clutched in one slender hand. David Hadison was sprawled in one of the metal chairs, glaring at his script, when she slid gracefully into one nearby.

He looked up, saw who it was, and grinned. "Just running over a little problem spot," he confessed.

"Is that what you're doing?" she queried with pursed lips. "I thought you were cursing the dialog."

He sighed. "Well, actually, I was. It isn't a very meaty part, darling. You have the only good lines."

"Want to trade?" she asked with a slow grin. "I'll let you borrow that big brown maternity dress I wear for the role."

He chuckled delightedly. "Cul wouldn't like it. I'm much too tall."

"How sad." She sipped her coffee slowly. "I'd offer you some, but you don't look like a coffee drinker."

"I'm a Coca-Cola man," he agreed. He put down the script, folded his arms, and stared blatantly at her. "Has anyone ever told you . . ." he began predictably.

Before he could finish, she stood up, threw her scarf royally over one shoulder, and fixed him with her best sharp scowl. "My good man, have the decency not to stare, if you please," she intoned with the crisp British accent she'd perfected. "We do not like our subjects making free with their eyes on our person."

He roared, clapping. "You do it with panache, darling," he said. "Elizabeth to the ruff."

She curtsied deeply. "We are pleased that you think so."

"How many times have you played her?" he asked as she sat back down.

"At least ten," she confessed. "Once in a nude play—I talked the director into letting me wear a corset."

He shook his head, studying her exquisite facial features—the dark eyes that were oddly gray, the flaming hair. "I've never seen such a resemblance, and I've been in the theater for ten years. You must be marvelous."

"I enjoy it, but it gets a bit tedious after a while," she confessed. "Although, she was a character. I doubt a woman's ever lived who was her equal, in statesmanship or just pure grit."

"You started out in Atlanta, didn't you?" he asked. "I saw you play in this very production about six years ago, just one time. You were magnificent."

"What were you doing in Atlanta?" she asked, curious.

"Trying to get a job in summer stock." He shrugged. "I didn't. I wound up in New York instead. It was a good thing, too."

"You're very good," she said genuinely, sipping her coffee as she studied him. "But aren't you Shakespearean, primarily?"

"By jove, yes, madam," he said with his own British accent and laughed. "I've done all of Shakespeare's plays at one time or another. But I'm trying to branch out."

"If the two of you can spare the time," a harsh voice rumbled behind them, "I'd like to start."

They got to their feet in a rush, noticing that the rest of the company was already assembled on stage, and Cul was nothing if not impatient. He glared at them as they joined the rest, and his mood didn't improve all morning. He snapped at Bett more and more, until by the end of the day she was practically in tears.

"Come on, darling," David said, taking her arm as she wrapped up against the chill to go out the stage door. "I'll buy you a nice cup of coffee."

"How about a sweet roll to go with it?" she asked with a wan smile.

"Whatever you like." He checked his pocket. "Well, almost."

She smiled gently. "Starving in garrets isn't what it's cracked up to be, is it?"

"How would you know?" he teased. "You're on top."

"Is that what I am? You really ought to come home with me."

"Can I?" he asked, all eyes. "I'll make the coffee."

She relented. It would be nice to have company, and she didn't really mind if David saw her deplorable apartment. He probably had one just like it. "Okay," she agreed, and went out with him, oblivious to the glittering green gaze that followed them.

It was a nippy evening, although it wouldn't be long until spring. Bett huddled into her tweed coat and led David up the long staircase to her apartment. The baby was crying, but the man who sang off-key was apparently resting his throat for the moment.

Bett opened the door and let David in with her "Well, as they say, it ain't much, but it's home."

"My God, you weren't kidding, were you?" he burst out, staring around him. "What happened?"

"I had a very inefficient business manager," she confessed. "He talked me into a bad investment, and also neglected to tell me about my taxes. I've got quite a bill with Uncle Sam." She shrugged. "They were very nice about it, in fact. I guess they get used to dumb people like me."

"I wouldn't call you dumb, not the way you act," he said kindly. He moved to the cabinet. "Is this the coffeepot?"

She glanced over her shoulder. "Yes. Isn't it the pits? But it works, all the same."

"Old-fashioned," he murmured, filling the basket with a filter and then dumping in a generous amount of coffee out of the can. "Boiling it on the stove."

"Well, coffee is coffee.

He sighed. "I guess so." He finished, turned on the burner, and sat down at the kitchen table across from her. "How did you wind up on the stage?"

"My mother convinced me that it was what I wanted to do," she said, laughing. "I was torn between acting and driving a semi, and she decided that it was more ladylike to act. Honestly, though, I guess it just came naturally. There was never anything else that I wanted to be. How about you?"

"Same thing." He made patterns on the table's chipped surface with a long finger. "I started out playing a squirrel in our third-grade play, and I was hooked. I've never wanted to do anything else. I studied and worked and eventually became the practically unknown actor you see before you."

"That's not true," she chided. "You were on one of the soap operas, I heard."

"For six weeks, until they killed me off." He propped his face in his hands. "I die well, you know."

"Yes, I know. Too bad you have to do it offstage in this play," she murmured on a laugh.

"I thought I'd do it with sound effects," he said with an evil glint in his eyes. "Screams and groans and thuds, that sort of thing."

"Cul would kill you," she suggested.

"He already wants to, I think." He watched her quietly. "But he's really after you, lady. I've never seen a director ride anyone as hard. What have you done to make him so antagonistic?"

"I breathe," she said simply. "It's something I'd rather not talk about, anyway. Would you like some cake to go with the coffee? I just happen to have two slices left."

"What kind?"

"Chocolate," she said.

He grinned. "My favorite."

She dished it up and he poured the coffee into the thick cracked mugs she'd found at a second-hand shop. "Isn't this fun?" she laughed as they sipped and ate. "There I was, living on Park Avenue in a luxury apartment, wearing leather coats and buying silk lingerie . . . and I never knew what I was missing."

"Must be hard," he said with real sympathy.

She considered that, stirring her coffee idly, with a spoon after she'd added cream. "Do you know, it isn't? I think I had my values all mixed up. Money and power and getting ahead were all I thought about. I've been noticing—forced to notice—how people live around here. It's pretty sobering. I think I've changed directions, all at once."

"Yes, it does make you think, when you see people so much less fortunate," he admitted. "I haven't had the kind of life you've had, not yet. But I hope that if I ever do make it, I won't forget who I was."

"I can't see you forgetting," she said, and meant it. "But you're supposed to say 'when,' not 'if,' you make it."

He grinned sheepishly. "Yes, I guess so. I get discouraged once a week and have to drown my sorrows in cheap wine."

"We all get discouraged, it comes with the territory. Just don't ever give up. Think through it. That's what I'm trying to do. I like to picture how it will be on Christmas Day this year." She sighed. "I'll have paid off my tax bill, I'll be in a hit play, and happy as anything."

"No man in that picture?" he asked softly.

She shook her head with a tiny smile. "Nope. I've never inspired a man to propose. I don't see it happening." Not ever, because of the scars Cul had left on her. But she wasn't telling that to a relative stranger.

"You might be surprised one of these days." He finished his coffee. "Well, I'd better run. If we're lucky we may actually get some sleep before rehearsal tomorrow. I didn't realize how late it was."

"Come again," she invited, her smile genuine. He was a nice man, and she liked him.

He nodded. "I'd like that. Good night, Bett."

"Good night." She closed the door behind his tall figure and sighed. It had been nice to have company.

After that, she and David became good friends. But their association had a devastating effect on Cul. He glared daggers at them every single day.

It didn't help that being around Cul was bringing back old, unwanted sensations. He could look at her and make her tremble. She hadn't counted on that reaction when she'd auditioned for the play. She hadn't counted on the fact that he might want to direct it himself. She should have thought it through.

One night as they were leaving the theater she stumbled over a metal chair, and Cul caught her just in time to keep her from having a bad fall. She looked up into his green eyes and saw an expression in them that made her heart run wild. His hard fingers on her back held her close for an instant, while his eyes went to her soft mouth and stared at it. It was like being kissed; she could almost taste his lips as she had so many years before.

"Getting careless, Bett?" he asked under his breath. "Don't fall, darling, it's not the kind of part you can do with a broken leg."

"I won't," she said unsteadily, and tried to smile.

He studied her slowly. "Come on. I'll drive you home."

"No," she said.

But this time he wasn't letting her talk him out of it. He herded her out to his Porsche and put her in the passenger side. Now what was she going to do, she wondered wildly. How could she let him see where she was living? The humiliation would be terrible.

"Come on, coward, direct me."

She drew in a steadying breath. "Queens."

He glanced at her, frowning. "I thought you lived on Park Avenue."

"I did, while I was making money," she said wearily. "I made a huge payment on my tax bill, Cul. I had to budget. The apartment—at least, my half of it—had to go."

"Were you living with a man?" he asked.

"Janet would hate being called a man," she said through her teeth. "And who I live with is none of your business."

"It was once. I almost asked you to move in with me, six years ago."

That was shocking, and her eyes told him so. "Me?"

"You." He glanced at her mockingly as he navigated a turn. "If you hadn't been a virgin . . ."

"Have you always had this hang-up about inexperienced women?" she asked bitterly.

"Just with you, oddly enough. I didn't want to take advantage of what you felt for me. Especially since marriage wasn't in my vocabulary." He glanced at her again. "It still isn't."

"Don't imagine I'm any threat," she said as coolly as she could, clutching her purse on her lap. "I'm a career woman all the way these days."

"You're an up-and-coming star," he agreed tautly. "I went to see you in that last Lewis play. You were good. Damned good."

"Thank you," she murmured, dazed. He didn't give praise easily. In fact, he rarely gave it at all.

"Now where to?" he asked.

"Left, then right at the next corner," she directed.

He pulled up in front of her apartment building and glared at it. He cut off the engine and pocketed his key.

"Cul, don't come up," she pleaded.

"I want to see."

There was no arguing with him. Resignedly, she led him up the long flight of stairs to the door of her apartment. His face was rigid as she unlocked it and let him in.

His green eyes swept the surroundings with obvious distaste. "My God," he breathed.

"There's nothing wrong with it," she defended, dropping her purse onto the couch. "It's warm and dry, and I have neighbors who'd come running if I screamed. Besides, if you remember, the apartment I had in Atlanta was much like this."

"That was different," he growled. "You were struggling then."

"I'm still struggling," she corrected him, turning away. "Would you like a cup of coffee, or are the surroundings just too much for you?"

"Is that how I sound? Like a snob?" he asked softly.

She glanced at him while she filled the pot and set it on the stove to boil. She got down the cracked mugs. "You were never a snob, Cul."

"I hope not." He pulled out one of the chairs and straddled it. He looked devastating, his blond hair gleaming in the overhead light, his eyes almost transparent in his dark, rugged face. "I was born to money, but I like to think I've never looked down on people without it. My circumstances were an accident. I could as easily have been born poor."

She'd forgotten until then about his background. One of his ancestors had been an English duke, and he had titled relatives. That straight, proud nose would have graced a family portrait, she thought, studying it.

The man who sang off-key had just started his nightly accompaniment to an opera recording, and Cul sat up straighter.

"Verdi?" he queried, frowning.

"Amazing that you recognized it." She laughed. "He has a lot of enthusiasm, for a man who can't sing. I've gotten quite used to hearing him."

"He probably dreams at night about a career with the Met," he murmured, not unkindly. "Not a lot of us get to fulfill our dreams," he added, and his eyes were brooding.

"What did you want to do that you haven't?" she asked as she poured the coffee. "You've made a name for yourself as a writer and a director, you have a play being made into a movie.... You've done it all."

"Have I?" He took the cup from her and watched her drop into a chair. "Not quite, Bett. There was one thing I wanted desperately that I never had."

"What?" she murmured absently.

"You, in bed with me," he said softly. His eyes wandered slowly over her face and what he could see of her body. "I wanted you to the point of obsession."

She felt the old hurt come back, full force. "How interesting. Was that before or after you humiliated me in front of the entire cast?"

He caught his breath at the ice in the calm little question. "Yes, I thought you were still bitter about it. I can hardly blame you. But at the time, it seemed the only way out." His eyes held hers, and there was faint regret in their green depths. "You were in love with me. Too much in love. I had nothing to give you, except a few kisses in the moonlight or, at best, a brief affair. I had to break if off."

"You might have just told me," she returned.

"You're a bulldog, Bett," he replied with a faint smile. "It wouldn't have worked. It had to be something drastic." He shrugged. "Gloria was willing and handy. I knew your pride would save you."

She laughed curtly. "Oh, yes, it sent me running for New York. Or hadn't you considered what the cast would do to me afterward?"

The smile left his face. "What do you mean?"

"Your 'girlfriend' made a huge joke about my hanging like an albatross around your neck. She made me the laughing stock of the entire company." Her eyes darkened with remembered pain. "I finally left because of it."

He drew in a sharp breath. "I'm sorry. I didn't consider that."

"No, why should you? I was handy, and you needed someone to amuse yourself with, wasn't that it?"

His eyes narrowed as he looked at her. "No. Walking away from you was one of the hardest things I've ever done."

"Were you so fond of juvenile adulation?" she asked with a laugh.

"It was more." He finished his coffee. "I'm a single, not a double, Bett. I'll live alone all my life, except for the occasional diversion. But not you." He watched her quietly. "Someday you'll marry and have those kids you used to dream about having. Three, wasn't it?"

Something odd in his voice touched her and she frowned. But before she could question it, he checked his watch and rose. "We'd better get some rest. Rehearsals are grueling, aren't they darling? Thanks for the coffee."

"Any time," she said lightly, showing him to the door.

He turned unexpectedly, and framed her face in his hands, watching it like some tawny cat. "You're as beautiful now as you were then, Bett," he said quietly, and his eyes were hungry. "Hair like wild honey... I used to dream of seeing it fanned out across my pillow."

Her lips parted under her roughened breath. It wasn't fair that he could still affect her this way. She felt the warmth of his big body and wanted to feel it against hers, wanted to drag that hard mouth down over her own and taste him just once again.

"That's something you'll never see," she managed tautly.

"Challenging me?" He drew her chin up and bent his head, opening his mouth just as it made brief, shocking contact with her own. "I don't have any more noble sentiments to protect you, Elisabet," he whispered. "Because you're not a virgin anymore. And frankly, darling, you'd be a pushover."

Even as he spoke, he was folding her into the curve of his body. His mouth opened hers, biting at it in the old remembered way, his own wild prelude to the deep, hot kisses he liked. Her fingers went to his chest to push, but lingered on the soft silk of his shirt under the sweater he was wearing. He had a mat of hair just over his breastbone. That one time in the park when they'd almost gone all the way, she'd felt it tickling her breasts just before it had crushed her into the soft grass.

"Cul," she moaned, and all at once her hands went up to hold him, her body arching into his.

He whispered something into her mouth, and his arms half lifted her against him while his tongue penetrated the soft dark recesses and made the teasing kiss into a declaration of possession.

She clung, moaning, drowning in the sensations, totally yielding. She was eighteen again, and Cul was her man, and she loved him, loved him, loved him....

He put her down abruptly, his eyes flashing. "No," he said on a harsh laugh. "Oh, no, little redhead, not again. I'm not going through it twice. Practice your witchcraft on Hadison, but keep your spells off me."

He turned, slamming out the door. She stared at it for a long time before she went back to put the cups in the sink. She lifted his, studying it with eyes gone soft and sad with love. Impulsively she brought it to her lips and kissed the place where his had been. There were tears in her eyes as she washed it.

If she'd hoped that Cul might soften, even a little, after that wild kiss, she was disappointed. He was as cold as winter stone with her the next day, tossing instructions around like bullets. Once she paused just a second too long before lines, and he went through the ceiling. It didn't help that she started getting involuntary stares from the rest of the cast. She was being ridden deliberately, and they knew it.

"What have you done to him now, darling?" David teased at the lunch break as she started out the door with her brown bag in hand.

"Still breathing," she told him with a smile. "Never mind, we're old enemies."

"Are you really?" he asked, his eyes openly curious.

She shrugged. "It doesn't matter. I'm off to the park for lunch. See you."

"Want some company?" he asked hopefully.

She shook her head. "Thanks, but I need to be alone for a little while."

He stared after her quietly, his dark eyes wistful and sad. She felt that long gaze, and almost turned around to invite him along. But what David was looking for, she couldn't offer. She had nothing to give him, not even half a heart. Everything she was belonged to Cul, whether he wanted her or not.

She sat down on a park bench and watched children play near the lake, smiling at their antics as they fed the ducks. She could have given Cul children, if he'd ever felt strongly enough about her. Once she'd thought he did.

The last time they were together had been on a day like this, she recalled, looking around at the blue sky and the warm sunshine on the grass. They'd lain together in a secluded spot in an Atlanta park under a spreading oak tree and talked lazily of fame and fortune and the future....

"What do you want to be, eventually?" she asked him, lying back in the grass. She was wearing a white peasant dress that day, with an elasticized bodice that showed off her golden tan. He was wearing his usual jeans and a burgundy knit pullover that day, a shade that emphasized his blondness.

His green eyes darkened as he let them run from her loosened reddish hair down to her long, slender legs where the skirt of her dress had ridden up over her knees. "Your lover," he murmured wickedly.

She laughed almost bitterly, her arms thrown back over her head as she closed her eyes. "That will be the day," she muttered.

She felt him before she saw him. Her eyes opened suddenly as his formidable weight settled over her torso, his forearms supporting him.

"How about today, then, Bett?" he asked softly, bending to her mouth.

They'd kissed before. Soft, clinging kisses. Even a few deep, hard ones. But this was a different way, an oddly sensuous way. His mouth nibbled and brushed and bit at hers in a slow rhythm that made her feel odd from the neck down. Her legs began to tremble as his

tongue traced the outline of her mouth and penetrated the soft line of her lips.

He lifted a little, easing onto one elbow so that his
other hand had free access to her body. It slid gently
over her waist for a long time before it moved up and
brushed lightly over her breast. She caught her breath
and he lifted his head, but he didn't move his hand.

He searched her eyes quietly. Seeing the yielding
fascination in them, he drew the elasticized bodice
slowly down until it rested beneath her breasts, bar-
ing them to the sunlight and his darkening eyes.

She held her breath, remembering how it had been.
The impact had been frightening; she'd never let a
man look at her like that. His eyes were narrowed,
glittering and spellbound by the swelling softness of
her.

Around them, the deserted park was quiet. Only the
soft cries of the birds interrupted the burning silence.

"Oh Bett," he breathed huskily. His fingers touched
the hardening buds as if it were the first time he'd ever
touched a woman that way, and they trembled. "Bett,
do you even know what it means, when this happens
to your body?"

She didn't, but he told her, in soft, sensuous whis-
pers as he bent to kiss them. She remembered crying
out just before his mouth came down to smother the
wild little sound. His hands took possession of her,
gentle hands that stroked and probed until tears were
running down her cheeks.

Her own hands were busy, trying to get his shirt out
of their way so that she could feel the thick mat of hair
over the warm muscles of his chest. With a shaky

laugh, he stripped it off and rolled onto his back, pulling her hands down to his body.

"Learn me, the way I've learned you," he coaxed, his eyes wild with passion as he watched her touch him, watched the fascinated wonder in her eyes as she explored him hesitantly, slowly.

"Don't stop there," he whispered when her hands trembled at his waist. He took her hands in his and moved them, and her breath caught at the harsh sound that broke from his lips.

The ground was hard at her back. The hardness of his body was like a brand, melting down onto every inch of hers in the shaded warmth of the day. His hands were under the dress, and only the sudden sound of people in the distance kept him from taking their lovemaking to its natural conclusion.

She could still hear the hard groan against her mouth, feel the trembling of his body as he rolled away from her.

The worst part of it all was that he had to put her back into her dress. She was trembling and crying too hard to do it alone.

"You mustn't," he whispered, rocking her against his bare chest. "It was beautiful. The way I knew it would be. We wanted each other, and that's all, it's so natural, Bett. Like breathing. There's nothing in the world to be ashamed of."

"I'm not ashamed," she whimpered. "I'm frustrated."

"Try to imagine how I feel," he murmured dryly.

She looked up at him and felt as if she had the world. He was looking down at her as if she were the most precious thing he'd ever seen, as if he loved her.

"Cul, I love you," she whispered to him as her pride yielded to the exquisite sensations he aroused. "I want to marry you and have your children!"

The glow of passion faded from his face. It was always this way whenever she mentioned children or anything permanent.

He framed her face in his hands and looked deep into her eyes. And then he kissed her, in a way he never had before or since. A cherishing, tender, utterly passionless kiss with his whole heart in it.

"Yes, I know," he whispered back. "I'll live on that all my life."

It was an odd thing to say. He helped her to her feet after he'd retrieved his shirt, and they walked back to her apartment hand in hand.

Shyly, she invited him to come in with her, but he shook his head.

"You're a virgin, darling," he said softly, brushing the long hair from her cheeks. "Despite the fact that I lost what little sense I had today in the park, I've got just enough left to walk away from you. I've nothing to offer you, Bett, don't you see?"

"I don't care about money..." she began fiercely.

"I know. Neither do I. But that wasn't what I meant." He bent to kiss her forehead with a tender brush of his mouth. "You deserve so much more than I can give you, darling. One day, you'll thank me. So long, Bett...."

And he'd walked away. She hadn't known it at the time, but he was walking out of her life. It was later that day that he'd announced his departure for New York, grimly, without looking at Bett. And it was that night that she'd discovered him with Gloria. From dream to nightmare, in only a few hours.

She felt tears in her eyes as she finished her sandwich and reached for her coffee. Her hand withdrew sharply as she recognized the man standing beside her.

"It brings back memories, doesn't it?" Cul asked coldly, glancing around them with his hands in his pockets. He was wearing his usual jeans, with a yellow knit shirt today, and she hated him for the powerful sensuousness of his body and the longing that had never died.

"Does it?" she asked blankly, staring carelessly at him with an acting ability that was surely Oscar quality.

He lifted his chin and studied her unsmilingly. "You can't act with me," he said after a minute. "I know you too well."

She laughed bitterly. "Yes, you know me." She picked up her coffee and sipped it. If she ignored him, perhaps he'd go away.

But he didn't. He eased into the seat beside her with a sigh, and stretched out his long legs.

"It's been a long day already," he remarked. "And we've hours to go. I hate damned rehearsals."

"Not half as much as I do, especially yours," she replied, throwing caution to the winds. She glared at him. "Must you make a career of humiliating me in front of the others?"

He laughed shortly. "I thought we'd come to that." He let his eyes wander slowly over her. "I want you, Bett," he said unexpectedly, and with cold anger. "I was sure that six years had blotted you out of my glands, but it hasn't. Ever since that night in your apartment, I've been walking around aching all over.''

Steady, girl, she told herself. This looks like a trap. She smiled carelessly. ''I'm sure you're not used to women refusing you, Cul, but I have a long memory. I'm still carrying your footprints along my spine.''

He searched her dark eyes quietly. ''It hurt me as much as it hurt you, walking away,'' he said. ''I loved you.''

That was something he'd never told her, even though she'd suspected it. To hear it put into words made her want to cry for all the lost years, the lost love. She turned her head away. ''Did you?'' she asked in a shaky voice, sipping more of her coffee. ''You had the strangest damned way of expressing it.''

''I didn't want marriage,'' he reminded her. ''I still don't. And there you were, with your adolescent dreams of marriage and children and happily ever after.''

She glanced at him. ''Well, pat yourself on the back. You escaped.''

''Yes, I did. But why haven't you married, Bett?''

She smiled poisonously. ''You cured me, darling. I'm not capable of emotional involvement anymore. Can't you see the scars, or is it just that you don't want to?''

His nostrils flared. ''Don't try to lay the blame on me,'' he said. He crossed his legs impatiently. ''You were the one with the dreams. I was honest with you from the beginning.''

''I was eighteen,'' she said. ''And you were the first man who made me tremble all over. I came of age with you. I learned what being a woman was all about.''

He lifted his head arrogantly. "Not quite."

She smiled slowly. "Well, not with you, of course," she continued, meaning to hurt. She felt a pang of triumph when his eyes narrowed and his jaw clenched. "My first lover wasn't quite in your league, but, then, beggars can't be choosers."

He was white in the face, but if he felt anything, it wasn't showing in those hard green eyes. He looked away toward the lake. "Did he hurt you?"

"Of course," she said, pretending a nonchalance she didn't feel. "But no one has since." She leaned back with the empty cup in her hand, sighing. "I suppose I should thank you for helping me over my inhibitions." She glanced at him, satisfied with the tenseness of his jaw. "That day in the park was an education in itself. Too bad the people had to come along when they did."

He looked at her, shocking her with the glitter in his eyes. "Yes, wasn't it?" he asked coldly. "But, then, the role of tutor never appealed much to me."

"Was that why you held back?" she murmured, watching him. "I always thought it was because you were afraid I might deliberately get pregnant, to hold you."

A strange, passionate expression crossed his face and darkened his eyes. He laughed mockingly and turned away. "You weren't the type to hold a man who didn't want to be held," he said in a husky tone.

"Especially after I had one of your lovers flung in my face," she agreed, standing, oblivious to the flash of pain in his eyes. "Never mind, it was a salutary experience. But not one I care to repeat."

"You didn't seem so reluctant the other night, darling," he reminded her, rising to tower over her. "In fact, you were clinging pretty hard for a woman who wasn't interested."

She managed a shrug with magnificent disdain. "It's been a long, dry spell between men," she said in a sigh. "Of course there's David..."

His eyes flashed at her. "Leave him alone," he said suddenly, unexpectedly.

"Dog in the manger, Cul?" she taunted.

She should have remembered his flash-fire temper. She'd pushed far too hard. He caught her arm and half dragged her into the sheltering tall bushes, jerking her against his body angrily.

"Damn you, Bett," he breathed as he bent and took her mouth.

This time she managed not to respond. His taunt had frozen her all over. Despite her resolutions, the sensuous roughness of the kiss made her hungry in a way that frightened her. She had to bite her tongue not to moan, clench her hands to keep them from reaching up to him. She wanted him, she loved him. But she was too afraid of him. He could reject her again, and she couldn't take it. It was better not to get involved in the first place.

It only took a minute for him to realize what she was doing. He lifted his head with a sigh, and glared down at her.

"Frozen over?" he taunted.

"That's right," she replied with a tight smile. "I don't want you anymore."

He breathed slowly, deliberately, as he let her go. He jammed his hands in his pockets and smiled mockingly. "I could persuade you, if I cared to go to the trouble. But you're not worth it, darling. I can have any woman I want these days. David's welcome to you."

He turned and walked away. Part of her was delighted that she'd routed him. But the biggest part wanted to sit down on the sidewalk and cry. Oh, Cul, she thought miserably, why couldn't you ever love me? I could be anything, do anything, if you'd just give me the chance. But he'd made it clear that his only interest in her now was physical, and she had too much self-respect to be made a convenience of. She picked up her bag and empty cup and put them neatly into a trash container, along with her memories.

Three

As they were going into the second week of rehearsals, Janet invited her to come to supper, but she couldn't ever seem to manage time off. Cul had stepped up the pace, and now David seemed to be on the firing line along with Bett. Cul had lost his temper the first time David muffed a line, and his constant criticism quickly produced more mistakes. She and David were spending a lot of time talking between scenes, and once or twice he saw her home. That seemed to enrage Cul.

But today, he was worse than ever, thrashing around the stage like an enraged bull. By the time they broke for lunch, Bett was actually shaking. It was her fault, and she knew it. Cul was still furious about the other day. He was going to make her life hell because of that lapse, and that was going to include anyone who even associated with her. It was no good. She was going to have to quit the play and find something else. She couldn't bear to see David humbled. He was a kind man, and it wasn't fair.

She went to Cul after the others left, watching him bend over a script with a pen. He looked up, his green eyes fierce and unfriendly.

"Well?" he growled. "Aren't you hungry?"

She folded her hands tightly in front of her and clenched them to give her courage. "I want out."

He rose slowly. "You what?"

"I want out. It isn't fair to David to be cut up just because he was friendly to me. Or maybe you're just looking for a way to make me quit. Either way, you've accomplished it. You win." She handed him her script.

But he stared coldly at her outstretched hand. "We're almost two weeks into rehearsals," he said. "I don't replace cast members."

"No, you just give them hell, don't you, Cul?" she asked wistfully.

"You wanted the part, darling," he said mockingly. "So did Hadison."

"Apparently that makes us guilty of some horrible crime," she replied. "I've told you I'm sorry I asked for the part. God knows, I'll never make the same mistake again. But if it means causing David to suffer, I'll—"

"He fluffed his lines," he said shortly. "So he caught hell. He'll catch it again, if he does it again. I want perfection here, not slipshod acting. I'll rail out anyone who doesn't do his job right, and that includes every actor in the cast."

"You've been singling us out!" she shot back.

"Maybe the two of you should pay more attention to practicing your lines," he said venomously, "instead of wallowing around in bed!"

She slapped him, quickly and deftly, without bothering to think of the consequences.

He didn't even flinch. He laid the pen down very carefully and caught her around the waist, jerking her against the length of his hard body.

"I've been waiting for that," he breathed, looking down at her. "Waiting, praying for a sign of your passion again..."

His mouth crushed down on hers, and all the years fell away. All of them, one by one by one, until she was a girl again and it was spring outside.

"Harder," he whispered against her trembling mouth. "Kiss me hard, the way you used to when we'd lie together in the park, on the grass, and you'd beg for my hands under your blouse. Do you remember, Bett?"

She did, she did, and her mouth was telling him so. She went on tiptoe, her arms clinging, her lips opening to the searching penetration of his tongue. She was on fire, blazing out of control, and his mouth was hard and warm and tasted of cigarette smoke and great passion.

He lifted his head, breathing roughly, his eyes searching hers in the hot silence. "Six years," he whispered, shaken. "And I touch you, and they all vanish. And I want you, even more than I did then."

She couldn't speak, couldn't breathe. Without another word, he bent, lifting her into his arms.

"We can't make love in comfort on the stage floor, Bett," he breathed with rough amusement, "but there's a soft, long couch in the office I'm using. Soft enough, and long enough, that we can lie on it together and pretend that we're as young as we were then."

"Cul..." she began in a whisper.

"No, don't argue, darling," he whispered back, brushing her soft mouth with his as he elbowed his way into the office and kicked the door shut. "Just let me kiss you for a few minutes, and take the edge off this damned hunger. I've almost gone out of my mind since the other night, Bett, I could taste you in my sleep! I want you, God, I want you!"

She wanted him, too, desperately, but it was only going to make things worse. She was still a virgin, although he wouldn't believe that, and she didn't want the complication of trying to manage an affair with him. She still loved him, damn him! Still, after all the years, all the humiliation. And she wanted him with a woman's hunger. But none of it was going to be enough!

"Cul, don't," she pleaded as he laid her gently on the long couch, his eyes running hungrily over the tight jeans and black blouse she was wearing.

"Yes," he said simply, lying down with her. "It's been a long time, but I haven't forgotten how your eyes cloud when you want me."

"We never went all the way," she reminded him shakily.

"You were a virgin, darling," he whispered. His fingers ran across one firm, soft breast and she trembled. "I couldn't take that from you, not when you might have married. Your husband would have wanted to be the first."

"But now?" she queried.

His hand cupped her warmly, his eyes watching the betraying motion of her body as he caressed her. "Now, you're twenty-five and no longer a virgin. And presumably, not wanting marriage. Now it's different. We can have each other. We can...love."

"Sex," she whispered, "is not love."

His eyes wandered back up to hers, and they glittered like sun-soaked leaves. "What we'll do together won't be a purely physical joining. There's too much between us for simple lust, and you know it." He bent his blond head and his mouth opened on her breast through the thin fabric. She arched, moaning.

"You cried the first time I did this," he whispered as he nuzzled the warm softness of her body. "We were lying under an oak tree in the park. I kissed you, and before you realized what I was doing, I had your breasts bare. My God, you were so beautiful! You started to protest, but before you could, I put my mouth here, like this." He kissed her there, softly, easing his hand under the blouse to lift it slowly, sensuously out of the way. Then his mouth found bare skin and a hard, throbbing nub, and her hands tangled fiercely in the hair at the back of his head and ground his mouth against her.

"It's the same," he whispered, stripping her out of the blouse even as his mouth found her again. "It's just the same, only you're more beautiful now, and you want me more. Help me..."

She found the buttons of his shirt and fumbled them open, helping him out of it. There had only been one time like this, that magical day in the deserted park, when they'd held each other so close and felt skin against skin and moaned with the aching need to have each other completely. But he'd held back, and none of her pleading words had swayed him.

"Yes," he whispered, grinding her breasts against the hair-roughened warmth of his chest. "God!"

Her legs were moving under his, she was on fire. It had been so long, so long, and she'd needed him so, and now all at once she could have him. He wanted her, he still wanted her!

"Now," she whispered mindlessly, her hands on his chest, lower, touching him in remembered ways, ways that drove him wild. "Now, please. Please."

"All of me?" he whispered back, lifting her hips up against his.

"All of you," she agreed, shaking.

His hands slid into the waistband of her jeans, onto her bare buttocks, his legs shifted between hers. "Look at me," he whispered.

She opened her drugged eyes as he eased down over her, letting her feel his hunger in an intimacy that ripped her apart with need. She cried out, a strangled, high-pitched little cry that had all of heaven in it, and he watched her with a face gone rigid in passion.

He moved against her roughly. "Now?"

"Yes," she ground out with a moan.

His lips parted as he watched her, and his hips ground into hers in a slow, sensuous motion. "Like this?" he breathed.

"Yes!" she whimpered, arching up.

"Here?" he whispered back, taunting her mouth with his.

She couldn't answer him; her mind was already picturing it, her body was crying out wildly for it.

He nuzzled her mouth. "First, I'll undress you. Then you'll undress me. Then I'll take you, right here on the couch...."

She whimpered again, her hips moving restlessly under the crush of his, until his hands caught and stilled them.

"Not yet," he breathed unsteadily. "Don't make me too hungry, or I may not be able to give you what you need. Now lie still while I get these clothes out of the way...."

He started to unbuckle his belt just as a door suddenly opened in the back of the theater and slammed heavily. His eyes looked down into hers and he cursed sharply.

"Damn!"

Her eyes closed as he rolled away from her and got to his feet. She couldn't move, the picture of seduction lying there with her blouse wide open, the pearly gleam of her breasts beautiful in the subdued light.

"As much as I love looking at you," he said softly, "you'd better button those buttons. We'll have company in a minute."

"Oh." She sat up, tugging at the blouse with fingers that shook. He knelt just in front of her and opened it gently. His eyes worshiped what he saw. He bent, taking one swollen nipple into his lips to suck it softly, warmly, moistly. Then, while she was taut with the wonder of the ecstasy, he brought the edges together and buttoned the blouse.

"Tonight," he whispered, looking straight into her eyes. "I'll take you home. And we'll love each other all night."

Tears welled in her eyes. She was too weak to tell him so. She loved him. It was like having every single dream come true, after all the long, empty years. How could she tell him no when she loved him? If one night was all she could ever have, wouldn't it be worth it?

"I feel as if I've waited all my life for you," he said, standing to straighten his shirt. His eyes searched hers quietly. "Every woman I've touched in the past six years has been you."

That admission brought tears to her eyes. He meant it; it was in every line of his face. And if he wanted her that much, couldn't it mean that he cared, just a little?

She stood up, brushing back her long hair, oddly shy with him. As the passion left her mind, it became sharp again and she remembered the pain of being pushed aside and wondered if she was strong enough to go through it again.

"Bett."

She looked up.

"Don't brood about it," he said softly. "Tonight, we'll talk. We'll make plans."

"What kinds of plans are there to make?" she asked sadly. "You'll take me to bed, and I'll let you, and in the morning, you'll be gone."

"No," he said. He drew her gently into his arms with a long, soulful sigh. "No. I'm no stronger than you are. The past six years have been pure hell. If we make love, it won't just be a one-night stand."

Her heart flew straight up. She drew back and looked at him with a hundred questions on the tip of her tongue.

He touched her mouth with a long finger. "Get rid of Hadison," he said, smiling. "You're my woman. Tonight, I'll even prove it to you."

She smiled. There was just enough time for that before noisy footsteps sounded in the hall, signaling the return of part of the cast. She went back to work with a fatalistic happiness. She'd never considered the possibility that she might want to sleep with a man without marriage. Well, maybe once, with Cul. But now, she had little else to look forward to. It was the way of the world, these arrangements. Marriage wouldn't make her any more committed to him than she already was. But a small ache deep inside her belied the smooth thought. She'd been raised to believe that people fell in love and got married and had children. It was going to be next to impossible to reconcile what she was contemplating with her conscience.

Nevertheless she put the consequences out of her mind and threw herself wholeheartedly into her role. Cul was obviously pleased, and even managed a kind word for David, which seemed to startle the poor man dumb.

Bett began to get nervous about nine-thirty, a half hour before Cul released the cast for the night. By the time the rest of them filed out, she was almost trembling with mingled anticipation and wonder because Cul was looking at her in a way he hadn't in six long years, and she was burning with a mad, helpless fever.

David paused at the door, glancing back until he saw Bett's eyes on Cul. With a look of sadness, David closed the door behind him. And they were alone.

"Afraid?" Cul teased softly as he led her out into the darkness.

"I don't know," she replied, tingling from head to toe.

"At least you aren't a virgin." He laughed, and she felt herself cringe at the laughter. "That's one problem we won't have."

He dropped his arm over her shoulders and pulled her close. "Bett, I'm on fire for you," he breathed as they neared his car. "It's all I've thought about for days." He turned her against the Porcshe and backed her up, so that his hips crushed her against the curve of the door and roof, letting her feel the wild hunger he'd just expressed verbally.

She could barely breathe as she looked up into his passion-darkened face in the streetlight. "I've dreamed of how it would be with you," she confessed shakily. "In bed, on cool sheets, with all the lights burning..."

He caught his breath, searching her eyes. "Is that how you want it?

"Yes, oh, yes," she whispered. "I want to see you while it's happening."

He groaned something, bending to kiss her slowly, roughly, with a hunger that made him tremble all over. "Let's go," he whispered, shaken. "While I can still find the strength to drive."

She sat beside him in a daze while he drove quickly to his penthouse apartment in downtown Manhattan. They stood rigidly together in the elevator. It wasn't until they were behind the locked door of the pent-house that he turned and looked at her.

"Do you want a drink first?" he asked quietly.

She shook her head slowly. Having waited six years, having made the commitment to him, she only wanted to be in his arms. She moved close, sliding her arms around him, pressing close with her eyes shut tightly.

"Cul...take a long time with me, all right?" she asked under her breath.

He caressed her back slowly. "I'll do my best," he whispered. His lips brushed over her closed eyelids, her nose, her lips. "I want you obsessively, Elisabet, but I'll be as slow as I can, all right?"

She smiled. "All right." She lifted her eyes to his. "Cul, I don't have anything," she said. "Can you...?"

He touched her mouth with his fingers and laughed with an odd bitterness. "Oh, yes, I can take care of it. Come on." He lifted her clear off the floor and carried her into the master bedroom with its beige carpet and chocolate-and-cream decor.

The bed was huge. King-sized, to fit a big man. He tossed her onto it and stood looking down at her with a tight smile on his lips, with glittering green eyes.

She sat up as he dropped onto the bed. He pushed her down again with a grin. "First things first."

He stripped, slowly, letting her watch him. She was fascinated, never having seen a man without clothes before. Her face, she knew, was hot with color, but she didn't look away. He was magnificent, like one of the photos in that magazine Janet had bought to show her, only much more sensuous. She couldn't look away.

"You aren't shy, are you?" he teased, drawing her to her feet.

"I think I am, a little," she confessed, touching his hair-roughened chest with obvious fascination. "We were never quite this intimate."

"We were in my mind," he said, and the smile faded as his fingers began to work at buttons and fastenings.

She stood very still, letting him ease away the fabric from her slender, high-breasted body. And when he was through, she looked at him as he studied her from head to toe with purely masculine appreciation.

"Has it been a long time since you've been with a man?" he asked.

"Why?" she asked nervously.

He touched her breasts with slow, tender hands. "Because if it has, I'll have to be a lot more careful with you, of course," he whispered, bending to kiss her. "You'd be... like a virgin for me."

Her lips parted shakily under his. "It...has been...a long time," she managed.

He smiled against her mouth and his hands went to her thighs to draw her body completely to his.

She caught her breath and moaned, and he smiled even more. His mouth parted hers with a tenderness that took her breath, and she felt a wild kind of shock at the contact with his hair-roughened nudity. She trembled all over from it, bursting with the joy of loving and being wanted.

He lifted her, placing her on the bed, then stretched out beside her. The lights were bright overhead, and she felt no shame at all as he looked at her and touched her. It was like dreaming, to be held and touched by him. And she loved him so... surely loving him was excuse enough to lay her principles at his feet, wasn't it?

She trembled wildly as he touched her in a new way, his eyes coming up to hers to watch her reaction.

He smiled again as his fingers probed gently and she gasped. "Oh, yes," he breathed. "Yes, I thought so, I was almost certain...." He bent to her breasts and nuzzled his face slowly against them, cherishing them first with his nose and chin and then, finally, with his warm, open mouth.

It was the beginning. In the minutes that followed, she learned things about herself and about him that made her explode with sensation and pleasure. He was so exquisitely slow that he almost drove her mad. She writhed helplessly, crying out, moaning, and all the time he watched, and watched.

Finally, when it was such torment that she was crying for fulfillment, his body moved over hers. He guided her, stilled her frantic movements, and all at once it was happening.

Her eyes flew open, agonized, straight into his, and he whispered, "Virgin." As his mouth came down, his body came down, and the ceiling seemed to come down with them as everything blurred into feverish motion and crashing pleasure and, at last, a shuddering kind of exhausted peace.

She felt his damp skin under her cheek after a few minutes, and her eyes opened, dazed, to stare across the swirls of hair just shades darker than that on his head. His chest still vibrated with the heavy beat of his heart, like her own.

His fingers smoothed her long, damp hair gently. "Did you save it for me, all those years?" he whispered.

"Save what?" she whispered.

"Your virginity," he replied. "Because, up until about ten minutes ago, you still had it. I knew."

She caught her breath. She'd thought she heard him whisper, but she'd been so wracked with pleasure that she hadn't been sure.

"You knew?"

"Umm-hmmm," he murmured lazily. "Do you mind if I feel unforgivably smug? I've never made love to an inexperienced woman before. And you didn't seem to be in very much pain," he added dryly.

"I wouldn't have known if I had been," she murmured, burying her face against him. "Cul, do you mind if I love you?"

"No," he whispered. "I don't mind. Because I've never stopped loving you."

She lifted her head, needing to see his face. And it was there, all of it, the passion and the tenderness and, yes, love.

"Then why...?" she began bitterly.

"Because you weren't old enough," he replied, brushing back the damp hair from her forehead to kiss it. "What we just gave each other is all I can offer you, Bett. I'm no more interested in marriage now than I was six years ago. I love you, quite desperately. But I can't marry you."

She searched his eyes. "I don't understand."

"I don't expect you to, darling," he replied. He rolled onto his side, tenderly drawing his fingers across her cheeks, her chin, in the lazy aftermath of passion.

He bent to kiss her softly on her swollen mouth. "There are reasons."

"Then what . . . what do you want?" she asked.

"I want to sleep with you, of course," he said, letting his hand wander slowly down her body until it made her leap with unexpected sensitivity. "All the time."

"For how long?" she managed in a last grasp at sanity.

"For as long as rehearsals last," he whispered as he bent and kissed her very slowly on the mouth. "Maybe for longer than that. Can't we just take it one day at a time, Bett?"

"Cul, I have to know . . ." she began.

But his body rolled onto hers and his mouth took possession of her parted lips, and the slow, rocking motion of it ignited new fires. It was almost dawn before they eventually slept, and she hadn't had the breath to ask any more questions.

It was just like Atlanta, only better. They were inseparable, something that David Hadison saw and reluctantly accepted. Bett was sorry for him, but too caught up in the fury of loving and being loved that she hardly noticed him for days afterward.

She and Cul went home to his apartment every night, and together in the big king-sized bed they made love in ways she'd never dreamed they could. As she grew more experienced and less inhibited, she began to notice that he wasn't taking any precautions. One night while they were watching a late movie on television, she mentioned it to him.

"I wouldn't mind if I got pregnant, of course, you know how much I want children," she murmured, feeling him stiffen. "But we're not really doing anything to prevent it."

He seemed to take a long time to answer, and she felt the rough rise and fall of his chest under her ear.

"Yes, you're right," he said finally, his voice oddly strained. "Look, we're almost through rehearsals, and I'm going to be in Hollywood for at least a month or so. You'll be in Philadelphia with the tryout. Let's cool it for a while."

She drew back and gaped up at him. He hadn't mentioned going to Hollywood, and her eyes widened with pure terror. Was he telling her that he'd tired of her, that it was over?

"Don't look at me that way," he said, his voice agonized. He caught her roughly against him, hurting her with the strength of the embrace. "God, don't look at me like that. I love you!"

Tears welled up in her eyes. "Then why are you walking out on me again?"

"I'm not," he breathed. His arms tightened even more. "You know about the play. I have to go out and finish work on the screenplay. And I have casting approval. I can't drop the project now. Besides," he sighed, drawing back to touch her wet face gently, "you're going to be busy yourself, getting geared up to win a Tony. Right?"

She smiled wanly. "Right." Her eyes searched his, fearfully. "You aren't breaking it off? I don't think I could bear it, Cul."

He swallowed, and his face paled. "It's just some breathing space, that's all," he said softly. He smiled down at her, although his eyes were oddly dark. "I love you, Bett. Believe that, at least."

"I do." She snuggled close to him with a long, relieved sigh. But if she could have seen the expression
on Cul's face, she might not have felt that relief. He
looked like a man being torn apart.

That was the first night he took her back to her
apartment. She didn't argue with him, his face was set
and he had that unbending expression on it. Besides,
perhaps he was right. When he'd spent a few late evenings watching the news and movies by himself, when
he'd done without her beside him in bed to warm him
in the cool night, he'd let her come back. She was sure
of it.

In the meantime, dress rehearsals began. The play
was ready to go out of town. Set designers were finished with the backdrops, all the props and costumes
were ready to go to Philadelphia. Everything was
loaded up and Cul said goodbye to Bett all too soon
when she drove him to La Guardia to catch his California flight.

"Write to me," she told him with bleak eyes as he
searched her pale face.

"Of course. Darling, you're so pale, are you all
right?" he asked softly, studying her.

"Yes, I'm fine. Just a virus. Janet had it, and I had
supper with her a couple of nights ago, you know."

"Take care of yourself. I'll be back before you know
it."

"I doubt that," she murmured. It was hard not to
cry. She felt as if something were ending, all at once.
Her eyes searched his frantically for signs that he still
cared, that this wasn't the end. But his eyes were un-
readable.

"So long, darling," he whispered, bending.

It was the most tender kiss they'd ever shared. She clung to him helplessly, needing his strength to support her. Her eyes watered with tears as his mouth softly probed hers, as his arms held her close, oblivious to passersby boarding the plane through the long ramp.

He drew back, his hands unsteady as he released her. "Be good, honey. 'Bye."

He gave her a last, wan smile, picked up his duffel bag, and walked down the ramp without looking back.

She went to her apartment feeling like death warmed over, and promptly lost her breakfast.

The infernal virus kept hanging on, sapping her strength. She managed to get through the tryout period, but it was the longest two weeks of her life. Fortunately the play was well received, without any changes being necessary. The stage manager had phoned Cul to tell him the good news about the audience's ecstatic reception.

"Did Cul have any message for me?" Bett asked hopefully.

He stared at her blankly. "No. I thought he'd have called you by now," he added with a grin. "You two were pretty thick when he left, weren't you?"

She managed a weak smile and turned away. So it was over. He'd have called or written if he'd meant what he'd said about loving her. He'd just wanted her. Now, with his appetite sated, he had no reason to continue the affair. By now there was probably someone else, some beautiful woman in Hollywood....

She sat down numbly in her dressing room. Why hadn't she seen the danger? Why had she trusted him? Damn her stupid heart!

That night, after the last performance, she went back to her hotel room and, in desperation, phoned Cul. She'd begged his number from the stage manager. It might be a terrible lowering of her pride, but she had to hear from his lips that he no longer cared, to believe it.

He answered the phone absently, as if his mind were on other things.

"Cul?" she said in a trembling voice. "How are you?"

"I'm fine, Bett," he said coolly. "I hear the play's going great."

"Yes, it is." She curled the telephone cord around her fingers. "Are you coming back for the opening in New York?"

"Afraid not, darling," he said carelessly. "I've got my hands full out here." He paused, apparently talking to someone in the room with him. "What's that, Cherrie? No, thanks, no more for me. Sure, the towels are in the bathroom, love, go right ahead." His voice was clear and sharp again. "Sorry, Bett, I've got company."

"Yes, so I heard," she said quietly, hanging onto the shreds of her pride. "I'm sorry I bothered you. Goodbye."

She hung up the receiver and cried as if her heart would break. Cherrie. At least she hadn't let him hear the torture she was feeling; she'd been very cool, very calm. Oh, God, why had she been stupid enough to trust him? Well, at least she knew the truth now, at least she'd been spared the humiliation of having him snub her in front of the cast. She got over him before, she'd do it again. Of course she would.

But she felt so weak that it was getting harder just to move around. David was worried about her, and showed it.

"Look, I've got a pal who just opened a medical pratice," he said when they were safely back in New York and a day away from the opening. "Let me take you to him, okay?"

She sighed wearily. "Okay," she agreed, resigned. "If you'll stop worrying. I think it's just emotional."

"Yes, I know you do," he muttered. "But I don't agree."

She went to the doctor, and sat motionless, not even breathing, when he began asking more specific questions.

Her jaw dropped. "You think I might be pregnant?" she burst out.

"Yes, I do," he replied gently. "There, there, it's not the end of the world. Don't you like children?"

Tears filled her eyes. "Doctor, I'm not married," she whispered. "I'm the leading player in a show that's opening on Broadway tomorrow night. I am dead broke, and the man who got me this way just walked out on me. Yes, it's the end of the world!"

He calmed her, had his nurse get her a cup of coffee, and spoke gently. "We'll have the results of the tests tomorrow morning. We'll know for sure then. Meanwhile, I'm giving you the name of a good obstetrician, just in case. And you'll need to get a lot of rest and eat plenty of protein."

She smiled wanly. "The end of the world," she murmured, and went out into the waiting room to join David.

"What did he say?" he asked as they walked down the street.

"I'm pregnant."

He stopped dead. "What?"

"He thinks I'm pregnant," she repeated dully. She laughed. "Cul just said a very definite goodbye, the play's hardly started, I have no money... Oh, David, I do have such a knack for fouling up my life. I loved him. That was my only crime, I loved him so much. Damn him!"

"You'll have to tell him," he said quietly. "I don't think you've got a choice in the world."

"Oh, he'll just love knowing what I've done," she grumbled. "Not that he isn't equally to blame," she added, remembering his careless attitude toward precautions.

"He has the right to know."

She glanced up at him. "I'm sorry if I've destroyed any illusions for you," she said, feeling oddly guilty. "I've loved him since I was eighteen. I couldn't help it, David."

"Of course you couldn't," he said, and held her hand protectively. He studied her wan face and smiled. "I'll take care of you. I'll even marry you, if he won't. How's that? God knows, we'll starve to death, but maybe the kid can learn to like fish and chips...."

She turned and hugged him, like a sister. "David, I love you," she whimpered.

"None of that," he grumbled, pushing her gently away. "I said I'd take care of you, and I will, but don't start making passes. And in your condition! I'm shocked!"

She laughed delightedly, clinging to his hand. "Well, there's still the one pale chance that I'm not pregnant," she said as they walked. "I'll just cross my fingers."

Crossing them didn't help. The next morning, the doctor's nurse called to tell her the test results. She was very definitely pregnant.

Four

Bett hung up the phone with a strange feeling of calm. Actually hearing it was different from imagining how it would feel. The sense of responsibility that came along with it forced her down into a chair, where she sat and stared blankly at the telephone.

Pregnant. Her slender hands touched her stomach lightly, protectively, and she looked down at it as if she expected to see the baby through it. She and Cul had created a human being. The thought was awesome. She caught her breath under its impact.

She'd wanted children ever since the day she met Cul, wanted them with the same wildness she'd felt with wanting him. It was, to her, such a natural part of loving that she accepted the fact of her pregnancy with quiet pride. Surely now he'd want her. Surely he wouldn't want their child born without a name. The only thing was, how was she going to tell him?

She sat down heavily on the sofa, her hands at her stomach, wondering at the miracle of life. A tiny smile touched her mouth and she sighed. A baby. After all the years of dreaming about it, it had happened.

She wondered if Cul would be as overwhelmed as she was. He'd admitted that he loved her, and surely it was true. How could he have been so tender if he hadn't? But in the same breath she remembered his slow withdrawal from her, the look in his eyes when she'd gotten upset about his going to California. And then, too, there was the girl he'd been talking to the last time she'd phoned him. Cherrie.

Her fingers traced an idle pattern on her now tight jeans. Cherrie. Was she a pickup, or someone he already knew? Oh, heaven, what if he'd been hungering for Cherrie and had taken Bett to bed out of frustration?

She got up and paced the floor. It had all seemed so simple earlier. She'd call Cul and tell him, and he'd be ecstatic and come rushing back home to marry her. But she was beginning to realize that it was more complicated than that.

He'd repeated over and over that he didn't want marriage, that he didn't want ties. Did she have the right to force him into it? If he didn't want fatherhood, mightn't it be better for the baby to just have the mother who wanted and loved him?

All the worrying made her tired. She crawled into bed and closed her eyes. She had a little more time that she'd begged off from Dick Hamilton, the stage manager. She'd use it to sleep. Tonight was opening night, and too much depended on her role now to blow it over concern for Cul's reaction. She'd worry abut that later.

She woke up still worried and undecided. She dressed hurriedly and went to the theater.

"Feeling better?" Dick asked, smiling at her from his perch on a chair backstage as technicians and prop people scurried around actors getting things set.

She smiled back. Dick was bald and fiftyish, with a comforting manner. Nobody could ask for a better manager. "Much better," she lied. "Just a bug."

He studied her. "Feel like going on?"

"On opening night? You've got to be kidding!" She laughed.

"Okay, let's get to it."

Everyone was nervous, even David. He stopped by her dressing room, with a pair of worn green socks in hand. "Feeling okay?" he asked with smiling concern.

She grinned. "Just great, thanks."

"Told Cul yet?"

The smile faded. "No."

"Don't worry, he'll be tickled pink," he assured her. He held up his socks. "My good luck charm. I never go out on opening night without them."

Her eyebrows lifted. "Do you wash them?"

He chuckled. "Well, yes, but the sentiment's there, all the same. What's yours?"

She sighed, tugging a tiny sterling silver cross out of her neckline and holding it up. "My mother gave it to me when I started summer stock. I never take it off through a performance."

"Actors are nuts." He chuckled.

"Eccentric," she corrected. "Cul always used to carry a turquoise key chain along with him. I suppose we've all got our little quirks."

"I suppose. Well, break a leg, darling."

"I'll do my best. You, too."

He winked and was gone. She sat staring into the mirror as she put on her stage makeup. Her heart hammered as she wondered if Cul would be out there tonight to watch. Surely he wouldn't miss opening night, even of a revival. If he came, then she could tell him after the show.

What if it wasn't a success? She frowned. No, that was defeatist thinking. Of course it would be a success. It was Cul's play, wasn't it? Would he bring Cherrie with him? Her heart fell. Damn men everywhere!

She was putting on the final touches when the door suddenly opened and Cul walked in, bigger than life in his dark evening clothes. The hand mirror she was holding slipped out of her nerveless fingers and hit the table with a clatter.

"Surprised to see me?" he asked.

"A little," she confessed. She wanted to get up and run to him, but the expression on his deeply tanned face was forbidding. "You look well."

"California is good for any ailment," he murmured, studying her carelessly. "Nervous?"

"I'm always nervous before a performance." She ran the brush through her hair again, trying to will her hand not to tremble.

"I tried to ring you this morning. You were out, so I called Janet. She said you were with David."

"Yes," she said noncommittally. "Did you want something?"

"To wish you luck."

"I make my own luck," she said, feeling suddenly strong and capable. She stared at him in the mirror. "How's Cherrie? Did you bring her with you?"

His face hardened. "Bett . . ."

"Don't worry, I'm not going to make a scene," she assured him. Her eyes searched his face.

"I never thought you were." He frowned, studying her. "You're different."

"I'm pregnant."

She hadn't meant to blurt it out like that; it was pure nervous reaction to his odd behavior. But it was too late for regrets. She watched him, trying desperately to find some kind of reaction.

He lifted an eyebrow over hard green eyes. "You're what?" he asked.

"Pregnant."

"Yes, I know. It's in the script."

She swallowed. "Cul, it's not only in the script. Not now." She searched his face, fascinated by the slow draining of color, by the sudden wild glitter of his eyes. She laughed nervously. "Well, I did mention that we hadn't taken precautions. . . ."

His breathing was ragged. Although he hadn't moved an inch, he seemed to grow taller, broader. His eyes were frightening.

"Pregnant by whom?" he asked in the coldest tone she'd ever heard.

"By you, of course," she faltered. "You know I was a virgin."

"Were, yes," he agreed. "But you've been with Hadison a lot since I left."

"I never slept with him," she said softly. "There was only you."

He started to laugh, slowly, bitterly. He threw back his head and roared, leaning back against the door, with his hands in his pockets. "So you're pregnant, and it's mine."

She felt an icy finger run down her spine. "Of course it's yours."

He caught his breath and the expression on his face could have stopped an armed combat veteran. "Well, that's interesting. A biological miracle."

"Miracle?" She stood up slowly, feeling her legs wobble. "We slept together!"

"Of course we did, darling," he drawled mockingly. His eyes narrowed, so cold they made her shiver as they ran down her body. "Just as I've slept with a dozen other women. But none of them got pregnant, and we never had to worry about precautions."

Her lips trembled. He wasn't making sense.

"You don't understand yet?" He lifted his head at an arrogant angle and smiled at her. "If you're really pregnant, Bett, and this isn't some wild last-ditch stand to get me in front of a minister, you've put your foot in it for good. You see, darling," he added, with ice dripping from his voice, "I can't father a child. One of the foremost experts in fertility in the country told me that it would take a miracle for me to get a woman pregnant. I'm sterile."

Sterile, sterile, sterile... The word kept echoing in her mind like a litany. He said something else, something insulting, but she wasn't hearing him anymore.

Her eyes were wide and horrified as what he was telling her penetrated the mists. He was telling her that he didn't believe the child was his. That it couldn't be his. But she knew for an absolute fact that it was, because there hadn't been another man!

"There wasn't anyone else," she whispered numbly.

"Of course not," he agreed. "And this is one for the record books, isn't it?" He shouldered away from the door. "But, Bett, if you tell anyone that baby's mine, I'll sue you to hell and back. I won't have my inadequacies paraded in a paternity suit and let the papers have a field day with me." His eyes glittered dangerously. "Beyond that, I'll make damned sure you never work again. So keep your lies to yourself, darling."

Her mind seemed to freeze. "But the baby..." she whispered shakily.

"That's Hadison's problem. not mine," he said, turning on his heel. "Let him take care of you."

"Cul!" she screamed.

He glanced at her from the open door, his look so contemptuous that it made her want to hide. "You never knew, did you, why I wrote so many plays about pregnant women? Or why I walked away from you when you were eighteen? You wanted children so much...." He laughed coldly. "I wish I'd had a camera when I told you. The look on your face was a revelation. Did you think I'd break my neck to marry you, once I knew?"

She knew her face was white, and she felt a wave of nausea wash over her. She sat down quickly, trying to breathe steadily.

"Not feeling well?" he asked mockingly. "I'll call the proud papa. I'm sure he'll be only too anxious to look after you. Break a leg tonight, Bett. I want you on that stage if you have to drag yourself onto it, understand?"

He walked out, slamming the door after him. She thought of every foul name she'd ever heard and used them all, with her head between her knees, until the nausea passed. She was devastated, but she wasn't going to let that animal know it. She'd go on, all right. And she'd give the performance of her life!

She got to her feet just as David walked in the door, looking pale and ragged around the edges.

"Are you all right?" he asked.

"I should be asking you," she replied, and inside she was numb and proud. "Did he hit you?"

"No. But he might as well have. My God, is he blind?" he asked curtly. "Why won't he accept the baby?"

"He doesn't want to be a father, of course," she returned smoothly. She couldn't tell him the truth, she didn't have the right. She took a deep breath. "David, I'm sorry."

"You have nothing to be sorry about, unless it's believing that fourteen karat s.o.b.," he said. "Don't worry, honey, I'll take care of you. We'll get married."

"No." She walked close and kissed his cheek gently. "You're like a big brother to me, and if you'll think about it, that's not a bad thing to be. I love him, David. I've never stopped and I never will, even though right now I could strangle him."

He laughed softly. "Want me to lend you a hand?"

She leaned against him. "No, never mind. But thank you, all the same." She closed her eyes. "David, thank you for caring."

He put his arms around her and held her gently. "I care a lot more than you want me to," he said softly. "Don't get upset. It's not good for the baby."

"Yes, I know." She nuzzled her face into his shoulder. "I'll be fine. Really I will."

"How cozy," came a harsh voice from the door.

They both turned to see Cul standing there, glaring. "You're being called. Let's get on stage, shall we? If you can tear yourselves away from each other long enough. It's curtain time."

"Shall we, darling?" she asked David, deliberately adding to Cul's already vivid picture.

"By all means." He took her arm and escorted her out the door.

She walked onto the stage at her cue with a presence she hadn't felt since she'd played Elizabeth the First. Her regal carriage, her confidence, radiated like fox fire. By the time she'd finished her monologue in the opening act, there was the silence of the tomb in the theater. But as the curtain went down on act 1, the applause burst like a bomb.

David hugged her ecstatically. "My God, what a performance!" he burst out backstage. "You're going to get the Tony for this!"

"Some performance." She laughed halfheartedly. "I'm a pregnant lady playing a pregnant lady. That isn't even acting."

"What you're doing out there is," he corrected, his dark eyes sympathetic. "I'm so proud of you, Bett."

She beamed. "Thanks. The show must go on, and all that," she added, although her heart was breaking into pieces inside.

"Doing okay?" Dick called, rubbing his bald head.

"Fine!" she called back, and he nodded and turned away.

She glared up at David. "Does he...?"

He grimaced. "Well, I was afraid he might push too hard, and that you'd let him. I know it wasn't my place, but dammit, somebody's got to look after you. Cul won't, damn him!"

She could have seconded that, but it made her feel odd, to have Dick know. Inevitably he'd let it slip, and then everybody would know. But she couldn't quit the play now. She needed the money too much.

"David, you're sweet, but..."

"Yes, I know." He bent and kissed her cheek. "I'll talk to you later."

He rushed off as she let the dresser put her quickly into a different, more definite maternity dress.

It was a long evening, and she tired more easily than she'd expected to. But the thought of Edward McCullough sitting out there in harsh judgment of her was enough to keep her on her feet even though she felt like lying down on the stage. She'd show him. His opinion of her didn't matter one bit! If he could believe she'd betray him with another man, he didn't have an ounce of trust in her. And that meant that he couldn't love her. Love was trusting, right down to the death.

She felt as if she'd been utterly used. But the baby was the one thing about their relationship that she couldn't regret. Even the prospect of raising it alone didn't bother her; she knew she'd manage. Cul was too frozen up to love anyone, but the baby would let her love it. She felt tears welling in her eyes. Why wouldn't Cul believe her? Why couldn't he let himself believe in miracles? Obviously he wasn't sterile, or how could she be pregnant? But perhaps he'd tortured himself with the thought for too long to let go of it. Like a bad habit, he couldn't break it.

Maybe someday he'd come to his senses, she thought. But by then, it would be too late. And there was the black possibility that he'd always believe the baby was David's, even if it grew up blond and green-eyed. By and large, people believed what suited them. And being a father obviously didn't suit Cul, because he couldn't face the possibility that she was telling the truth.

When the final curtain went down, she was utterly exhausted and ready to drop. But she walked out to thunderous applause and was pelted with long-stemmed red and yellow and white roses, and bouquets of them were carried onstage. Tears ran down her cheeks as the opening performance ended triumphantly. Her career was made. The money would come. Her financial worries were over. But her personal ones were just beginning.

Backstage in her dressing room, she took off her makeup and dressed in slacks and a pullover blouse before people managed to break in and start congratulating her. She took it all with breathless enthusiasm, feeling unexpectedly buoyed up and adored.

It wasn't until Cul showed up with a devastating blonde in tow that the bubble broke. And David wasn't around to catch her this time.

"You were just wonderful, dear," the blonde said from her exquisite mask, clinging to Cul's arm. "I wanted to be an actress, you know, but mother wouldn't hear of it," she added on a carefully sad sigh. "I did enjoy your interpretation of the role. Cul said you were a good actress, but I have to be shown. Of course, I was. I truly was."

"Thank you," Bett said politely, wondering what the blonde would say if she told her about the baby and who its father was.

"Now we really must go," the blonde told Cul, "if we're going to make it to Nassau tonight. Cul's spending a few weeks with us while he works on that Hollywood thing, aren't you, darling? Not that I expect him to do much work around me," she added suggestively.

"Keep the quality up, Bett," Cul said with careless praise. "You were extremely good tonight.'

"Don't bother your head about me, darling," Bett said with sarcastic emphasis, "I'm a survivor."

He glared at her. "Yes, I found that out, didn't I?"

She only smiled. "I'll see that you get an invitation to the wedding," she said, lying deliberately because he was killing her and she wanted to hurt him just as badly.

But there was no reaction at all. He lifted his eyebrows. "Do that. I might be able to make it. Ready, Tammy?"

The blonde started to say something, but he pushed her gently out the door. "Not now, darling," he murmured on a laugh. "So long, Bett."

And just that quickly he was gone. She sat down. Cherrie. Tammy. So that was what Cul's women usually looked like. Exquisite and wealthy and cultured. Everything that Bett wasn't. She felt the tears come with a sense of desolate finality.

She grabbed her coat and ducked through the well-wishers, rushing until she reached the stage door. She thought she heard David call to her, but she ignored him. Her mind had been crushed by Cul's behavior, by his deliberate mocking of her condition, and by the fact that he'd brought that woman with him.

She wasn't even aware of where she was going. She didn't know or care that it was dark and cold, and she found herself heading for the river.

She walked for a long time, keeping her pace brisk, oblivious to the danger. She felt her feet go numb with every step, and in her mind Cul's voice kept repeating, "I'm sterile.... I'm sterile.... The baby isn't mine...."

Around her, the sound of traffic sounded unreal. Her eyes noticed the lights without really seeing them. She'd found the river, and she was so numb with pain and hopelessness that she didn't even think about the baby she was carrying. She stared down at the black water, wondering if there was any peace to be found there.

In a moment of insanity, she started to jump.

"Bett! No!"

The wrenched agony in that voice stopped her. She blinked, turning, to see David running toward her furiously.

"David?" she mouthed.

He had her. He dragged her into his thin arms and held her, trembling with reaction.

"You fool," he choked breathlessly. "You silly little fool!"

Tears ran down her cheeks as she let the emotion overflow and felt, for the first time, the impact of Cul's rejection.

"He doesn't think it's his baby," she whispered brokenly. "He brought that blond aristocrat to flaunt at me, and he said . . . he said . . . I was a tramp!"

"And you know it isn't true," he told her, holding her closer. "You crazy little girl, didn't you think about the baby? My God, if I hadn't been worried to death and come after you, I shudder to think what might have happened!"

She cried helplessly, clinging to him. "I can't bear it," she whispered. "It was bad six years ago when he walked away, but it's killing me now! It's killing me, David. I love him, I love him so!"

He drew in a ragged breath and bent his head over her. "Here, this is no place to stand around after dark. Come on, we'll take a cab home."

"Can you afford a cab?" she managed, wiping at her eyes with the handkerchief he pressed into her hands.

"No, of course not," he assured her. "But we're taking one all the same. At the end of the week, we get paid. I'll just eat hot dogs until then."

"I can fix you something to eat," she offered gently.

"Real food? No cardboard?"

She managed a smile and clung to his arm. "No cardboard. How about some eggs and bacon?"

"Sounds great! Lead the way."

She was silent back to the apartment. She cooked in a daze, wondering at the numbness inside her, horrified at the moment's insanity that had threatened her life and the baby's. Her hand went slowly to her stomach.

"You're all right," David said as he watched her. "So is the baby."

"Yes, but it doesn't seem real at all, what I thought of doing. I'm not a suicidal person, you know, I'm very strong." She glanced at him with tortured eyes.

"We're none of us superhuman, and you'd had a nasty knock," he reminded her. "Add to that the excitement and tension of opening night. It's no wonder you went a little mad. Under the circumstances, it's even understandable."

"If it hadn't been for you, I might have jumped," she said softly.

"Maybe you'd have come to your senses in time," he offered consolingly.

"I don't know." She turned off the flame under the eggs and slid them onto a platter with the bacon and toast. "I've never had that happen before. I didn't even realize what I was doing."

"You need a little rest," he told her. "Before long, it will be Monday. I'll take you to the park."

"No!" she burst out, her face white.

"I'll take you to a movie," he said quickly. "That new sci-fi thriller. Okay?"

She sat down, catching her breath. "That might be nice. I like science fiction."

"So do I. See, already we have common interests. Why not marry me while we look for more?"

He was teasing, but she sensed a willingness under it, and she was tempted to say yes, to lay her burdens on his thin shoulders and let him take care of her. But it wasn't fair. She couldn't give him what he wanted from her, and it was no use pretending. She couldn't deliberately hurt him.

"We'd both starve to death, then," she replied lightly, smiling at him. "I can't eat cardboard."

"I could cut out magazine ads," he offered, brightening.

"The baby wouldn't like it."

"You'll have to be a firm parent and tell him to cool it," he returned.

She laughed. It was as if the baby was already a person. "I'll call him Buick," she threatened.

He blinked. "Buick?"

"Well, I've always wanted one...."

He burst out laughing. "Shame on you!"

"Okay, I guess it wouldn't be quite fair." She thought for a minute. "How about Jason? Isn't that a nice name? I'll call him Jason Clarke."

"What if she's a girl?" he asked.

"I'll call her Jackie," she returned. "But she won't be a girl."

"You're sure of that?"

Her eyes clouded. "Cul was an only child, but his mother had two brothers, and his father was one of six boys. Yes, I'm ... reasonably sure."

He sipped his coffee. "Where did you learn to cook like this?" he asked, changing the subject.

"At home, when I was twelve. Mama said girls should know how to cook." She leaned back, losing herself in memories of her childhood, in the peace of the years before she'd met Cul. All too soon, it was bedtime and David was saying good-night.

"I'll sleep on the couch, if you like," he offered, frowning at the door.

"I'll be all right," she assured him. "I'm quite through trying to leap off bridges. Cul would probably celebrate, not grieve, so the only person I'd hurt would be the baby. I won't do that again."

"Good girl. Sometimes a good night's sleep makes all the difference. I've seen it keep one of my friends from jumping off a building. Much harder than water," he added with studied lightness.

"As you say. Thanks for being my friend, David," she said gently, and reached up to kiss his lean cheek.

"My pleasure." He touched her face softly. "Good night, Elzabeth the First. I like your spunk."

"I almost lost it, didn't I? But never again. I'll have this baby," she told him, smiling with determination. "And I'll never let Edward McCullough so much as touch it, or me. Revenge is sweet, don't they say, and someday he'll want me. But he won't have me."

He nodded. "I know you're pretty cut up right now, Bett," he said gently. "But it will pass. Just hold on to that, if you can, and get through it."

"Is that how you do it?"

He nodded. "You always think of Christmas, don't you?" He laughed self-consciously. "So we'll hold on until Christmas. Everything will be fine."

"Thanks."

"Get some sleep. I'll come by for you in the morning."

"David," she began worriedly.

"Hush. I've got a lot of love to give somebody, why not you and the baby?" he asked quietly. "I won't ask a thing of you."

"It's not fair," she whispered.

"Life never has been," he agreed. "But people who never risk, never gain. Not in any big way. If Cul ever comes back, I'll step aside. But if he doesn't . . ."

"He won't," she said, turning away. "But I can't give you what I can't feel, and I don't want to hurt you, David. I've been hurt enough to know how it feels."

"I'd rather be hurt by you than kissed by anyone else," he said curtly. "Now get some rest. I'll see you in the morning."

He turned and walked away. She watched him as far as the elevator and then slowly closed and locked the door.

Five

Janet came over to cook breakfast for her the next morning, her arms full of papers.

"David said you'd been ailing," she said cheerfully, "so I came to play mama. Your reviews are fantastic. You've made it, honey."

"Have I ever," Bett sighed. She sat up, turned white, and dashed for the bathroom, barely making it in time.

When she came back out, Janet was staring at her over a platter of scrambled eggs, her face concerned.

"Yes, I can see you've been ailing," Janet said softly. "Poor darling. Poor, poor darling. Does he know?"

She nodded miserably.

"Well, is he going to marry you?"

She shook her head.

Janet made a rough sound in her throat. She slammed down the platter of eggs. "Why not?"

"He doesn't think it's his."

"Oh, baloney." Janet sat down beside her on the bed, pulling the tear-washed face onto her shoulder. "Why doesn't he?"

"You can't ever tell anyone."

"Dearest friend, when have I ever told anyone anything?"

Bett smiled wanly. "He says he's sterile."

"Cul?"

"Cul." She sighed wearily. "Janet, he thinks I've been sleeping with someone else. He's positive it isn't his, he won't even discuss the possibility. I don't know who told him he couldn't father a child, but, boy, have I got a shock for whoever did!"

"Yes, obviously. What are you going to do?"

"Have it."

"I figured that. I mean, how are you going to manage?"

"The play's a hit, and I'm making money, real money. I can pay my taxes." She sighed. "I'll stay on here and when the time comes, I'll check myself into a hospital and have the baby. Then I'll worry about diapers and baby-sitters and such." She smiled. "Janet, I've wanted all my life to be pregnant. I loved him, you know." Her voice broke. "If I can't have him, at least I can have the baby. And I'll love him, and take care of him, and give him all the adoration I can't give to his father. I'll make out just fine. I'll have more than most people ever manage."

Janet studied her quietly. "Yes, I guess so. But it's such a mess."

"David offered to marry me."

"Great. You can starve together," Janet chuckled. "He's a nice man."

"Yes. But I don't love him." She brushed the hair away from her face. "He can be the baby's uncle."

"Can I be his aunt? We'll have a christening and everything."

"That sounds super." She pulled herself up and went to the window. "It's starting to look like spring. And by Christmas, I'll have a really special present, won't I?"

She turned, and the radiance on her face made Janet smile. "A special present," she agreed. "Now, how about some scrambled eggs?" she asked, rising. "You need lots of good food now, to keep you both healthy."

"Sounds terrific. I'll just get the ketchup."

Janet gritted her teeth and spooned the eggs onto plates.

As the days went by, Bett hardly had time to feel sorry for herself. The role took up most of her time. The play was performed Tuesday through Saturday evenings with matinees on Wednesday, Saturday and Sunday. Monday was her only day off, and she usually spent it with David and Janet.

The two of them astonished her. Neither was a mother-hen type, but they seemed determined to protect her from life at large. It had stopped being her baby and became everybody's baby. Inevitably the day came when the rest of the cast realized what was wrong with Bett. That was when the trouble started.

An enterprising reporter for one of the local papers managed to get the information without asking Bett. He published it. The entertainment page carried the blatant headline: "Fantasy Becomes Reality—Pregnant Woman Plays Lead in McCullough's *Girl in a Dark Room.*"

Bett almost fainted when she read it. The article was full of praise for the idea, preconceived it seemed, of having a pregnant girl play the role. The reporter went on to speculate that when Bett delivered, her understudy could handle the role while she was out having the baby. Of course he didn't mention the baby's parentage, tastefully leaving it as part of the mystery.

Although Bett was furious, David wasn't. He thought it was terrific.

"Besides," he said, while the three of them lounged at a sidewalk café and sipped coffee. "It's giving us some great publicity. And it keeps you from pushing yourself too hard."

"How could I manage to do that?" Bett asked with a sour face. "Everybody in the cast hounds me to rest."

"You're looking great," David grinned. "All creamy and smooth and healthy."

Janet looked at the slightly rosier, healthy face and giggled. "Very healthy," she added.

"Just because I can't zip up my slacks or button my normal blouses is no reason to call me fat," she told them, and defiantly ordered a cream puff for dessert.

Nobody had heard from Cul. The first two weeks were over, a roaring success, and it was nice to have this Monday off, to breathe. Bett finished the cream puff and dusted off her fingers.

"Too much of that isn't good for you," Janet mentioned.

"And you need to walk more," David agreed.

"Well, I'll stop eating cream puffs, and I'll walk right now," she promised, holding up a hand when they tried to rise. "I'm a big girl, and no puns, I can walk alone. See you all later."

"We're coming for supper," Janet reminded her.

"By all means, we'll have pickles and yogurt mixed with mashed potatoes," she said, grinning.

Janet quickly sipped her coffee, and David groaned. Bett left them sitting there. The two of them looked so right together, she thought, glancing back. Maybe that might work out one day. She shuffled along from window to window, enjoying the luxury of free time. The last week of dress rehearsal had meant twenty-hour days, and she'd been tired already. Now she was picking up, feeling healthy. The doctor had given her tablets for the morning sickness. Although she didn't take many of them, she found that the occasional one made it easier for her to get around. And one of those multiple vitamins he'd prescribed made her feel capable of lifting a truck.

She was already feeling heavy, despite the fact that she hadn't started to show at all. Her pants had stretchy waistbands, so they weren't too tight, and she wore bigger bras and looser blouses. The one she had on today looked just right for early spring. It was white cotton, with a V neck, and felt lacy and feminine. She wore blue slacks with it, and left her hair long around her shoulders. She felt young, and full of

Take 4 Books
–an Umbrella & Mystery Gift–
FREE

And preview exciting new Silhouette Desire novels
every month—as soon as they're published!

Silhouette Desire®

Yes…Get 4 Silhouette Desire novels (a $9.00 value), a Folding Umbrella & Mystery Gift FREE!

Elaine Camp's HOOK, LINE AND SINKER. Roxie Bendix was a reporter for *Sportspeople.* Sonny Austin was the country's top fisherman and the subject of Roxie's next interview. It wasn't long after they'd met that Roxie knew she would pay any price to make sure Sonny would not become the one that got away.

Diana Palmer's LOVE BY PROXY. When Amelia Glenn walked into Worth Carson's board room wearing only a trenchcoat and a belly dancer's outfit, she was determined to do her act. Worth had her fired, but Amelia didn't know that the handsome tycoon was determined to bid for her on his own terms!

Joan Hohl's A MUCH NEEDED HOLIDAY. For Kate Warren, Christmas was a time of emptiness—until she met handsome Trace Sinclair. And what had been a contest of wills began to change into something else, something only their hungry hearts dared admit…and would not let rest.

Laurel Evans' MOONLIGHT SERENADE. Emma enjoyed life in the slow lane, running a radio station in a small town. So, when TV producer Simon Eliot invited her to give a speech in New York she refused. So, why did Simon keep returning on weekends? And why did Emma wait so desperately for his arrivals?

SLIP AWAY FOR AWHILE…Let Silhouette Desire draw you into a world of real-life drama and romance as it is experienced by successful women in charge of their lives and careers, women who face the challenges of today's world to make their dreams come true.

EVERY BOOK AN ORIGINAL…Every Silhouette Desire novel is a full-length story, never before in print, written for those who want a more sensual, more provocative reading experience. Start with these 4 Silhouette Desire novels—a $9.00 value—FREE with the attached coupon. Along with your Folding Umbrella and Mystery Gift, they are a present from us to you, with no obligation to buy anything now or ever.

NO OBLIGATION . . . Each month we'll send you 6 brand-new Silhouette Desire novels. Your books will be sent to you as soon as they are published, without obligation. If not enchanted, simply return them within 15 days and owe nothing. Or keep them and pay just $11.70 (a $13.50 value). And there's never any additional charge for shipping and handling.

SPECIAL EXTRAS FOR HOME SUBSCRIBERS ONLY . . . When you take advantage of this offer and become a home subscriber, we'll also send you the Silhouette Books Newsletter FREE with each book shipment. Every informative issue features news about upcoming titles, interviews with your favorite authors, even their favorite recipes.

So send in the postage-paid card today, and take your fantasies further than they've ever been. The trip will do you good!

CLIP AND MAIL THIS POSTPAID CARD TODAY!

NO POSTAGE
NECESSARY
IF MAILED
IN THE
UNITED STATES

BUSINESS REPLY MAIL

FIRST CLASS   PERMIT NO. 194   CLIFTON, N.J.

Postage will be paid by addressee

Silhouette Books
120 Brighton Road
P.O. Box 5084
Clifton, NJ 07015-9956

Take your fantasies further than they've ever been. Get 4 Silhouette Desire novels (a $9.00 value) plus a Folding Umbrella & Mystery Gift FREE!

Then preview future novels for 15 days—
FREE and without obligation. Details inside.

Your happy endings begin right here.

Silhouette ❦ *Desire* ®

Silhouette Books, 120 Brighton Rd., P.O. Box 5084, Clifton, NJ 07015-9956

☐ YES! Please send me my four SILHOUETTE DESIRE novels FREE, along with my FREE Folding Umbrella and Mystery Gift, as explained in this insert. I understand that I am under no obligation to purchase any books.

NAME _____

(please print)

ADDRESS _____

CITY _____ STATE _____ ZIP _____

Terms and prices subject to change.
Your enrollment is subject to acceptance by Silhouette Books.

SILHOUETTE DESIRE is a registered trademark.

CTD076

hope. Despite the fact that Cul had almost dealt her a death blow, she was coming slowly back to life. People around her were kind, especially since the article. And although nobody really knew who the father was, most people agreed that it was a toss-up between David and Cul. Considering their respective behaviors, they'd narrowed the choice to David. He was so attentive and proud, who else could the father be? Bett only smiled. She was happy with her pregnancy. She hadn't told her parents yet, but she felt that she'd be able to make them understand. And since she was living in a city the size of New York, hardly anyone would notice the lack of a husband. Her parents could tell their small circle of friends what they liked.

She walked around the corner to her apartment and stopped dead when she saw the black Porsche sitting in front of the building. There was nobody in it, but she knew whose it was. Her eyes went up the wall to her apartment.

For a minute she debated whether or not to go up. She wanted to see him, needed to see him, to feed her starving heart. But wouldn't it only make it worse? She stood indecisively.

The apartment house door opened and Cul walked out. His blond hair was ruffled by the wind, and he was wearing beige slacks with a white turtleneck sweater under a tweed jacket. He stopped, spotting her instantly, and then started down the steps toward her.

She didn't run. She stood quietly with her hands in the pockets of her sweater and waited, very calmly.

He came to a stop just in front of her, his eyes involuntarily going down to the front of her loose blouse.

"Who leaked that story?" he asked curtly.

"I didn't, in case that's why you've come looking for me," she returned with equal frigidity. "I have enough troubles without broadcasting my condition. I've worried every night that my parents might somehow get a copy of that paper."

He stopped just in front of her, his face quiet and curious, his eyes bleak. "You don't look well, Bett."

"I'm pregnant," she reminded him haughtily. "The early stages are uncomfortable for some women."

He drew in a slow breath and stuck his hands in his pockets. "You're going to keep it?"

"Of course," she said quietly.

"Is Hadison pleased?"

It was an offensive, sarcastic thing to say. But from his point of view, probably justified, she thought miserably. He was sure that it wasn't his. A doctor had told him he couldn't father children. Probably the doctor didn't believe in miracles, but Bett did. She was carrying one.

"David isn't the father of my child," she told him.

"Then who is?" He asked mockingly. "The milkman?"

"My baby is none of your business," she said with cool pride. "I'm being taken care of by just about everyone except the baby's father."

"Didn't he want it?" he asked curtly.

"It's yours, Cul," she replied with venom in her whole look. "You can deny it until hell freezes over, but it won't change facts! I'm sorry you won't believe it, but it's the truth!''

"Didn't you hear what I told you?" he demanded hotly. "I said, I'm sterile, Elisabet. Don't you understand? I couldn't father a child, no matter how hard I tried! That baby you're carrying isn't mine!"

"Then whose is it, since you're the only man I've ever slept with?" she threw back.

"Hadison's," he said cuttingly. "He's been hanging around you ever since we began production."

"He's my friend, and I like him very much, but I've never slept with him. I never could."

He laughed disbelievingly. "Sure."

"Is it so impossible for you to accept that your doctor could make a mistake?" she asked furiously. "We're all human! The lab that did the tests could have inadvertently switched them, or a technician could have read them wrong!"

"I never made any other woman pregnant," he said shortly.

"Most of the women you hang around with are on the pill," she shot back, "and you know it. How many of them were unprotected?" She laughed up at him. "You and your women. How many do you have now, Cul? You must keep scorecards, so that you don't lose track of them!"

"You're one to talk about scorecards, you tramp," he bit off, stung by the contempt in her voice into striking back.

She slapped him as hard as she could, watching fascinated as the red imprint of her hand burned on his hard cheek. He didn't even flinch. He just stared at her.

"There was no one except you," she said in a shaking tone. "Never anyone except you. I loved you!"

His eyelids flinched, just a shadow of movement. "Did you?" he taunted. "Then why take a lover on the side?"

"I didn't," she said fervently, trying to make him believe. But it was hopeless. She could see it in his face. "Oh, why won't you believe me?"

"I wish I could," he said quietly. "You don't know how much I want children, Bett, or what I'd give to have fathered that child you're carrying. But I don't believe in miracles. You should have accused someone less cynical than me."

"Have I ever lied to you?" she asked sadly.

He shrugged. "How would I know? You're an actress, darling."

"This isn't acting," she told him, touching her belly. She searched his face, but there was nothing there. He was adept at hiding his emotions, if he even had any. She'd never felt more helpless. "Well," she said after a minute, "you were looking for a way to get rid of me, weren't you? This just helped you along."

"Are you sure of that?" he asked, his eyes level and unblinking. "How do you know what I feel?"

"No one does. You hide it very well, don't you?" she asked bitterly. "I'm not quite that experienced yet. I was a pushover. I'd wanted you for so long. I was foolish enough to think that you had some feeling for me. But you never did, did you? It was all just physical with you, from the beginning."

"Not quite," he said through his teeth. His eyes went down to her belly and narrowed. "I was on the verge of a proposal. I missed you those weeks I was away." Missed her, he mused bitterly. Ached for her! "I was just inches away from falling in love with you."

"Was that before or after Cherrie and Tammy?" she asked politely. "You can accuse me of running around on you, but you're the one with the entanglements. A new woman every night. Amazing, that I lasted so long!"

"Don't," he said gruffly, turning his eyes toward the street. "Don't make it sound cheap."

"Wasn't it? You were just passing time. I was nothing more than an outlet for your needs, and I was too besotted to know it. Well, at least I won't spend the rest of my life agonizing over you, Cul. It's rather a blessing that this happened."

"I'd hardly call unwed parenthood a blessing," he returned.

"But then, you don't need any stability," she told him. "I do. I need love."

"Did you love the baby's father?"

"As a matter of fact, I did," she sighed, smiling wistfully up at him. "Idiot though you are."

"It isn't mine, and wishing won't make it so," he said coldly.

"That's what they say, all right." She pulled her sweater closer around her, feeling the chill of the wind right through her. "Well, I'm sure you must have a woman waiting somewhere, and I'm not supposed to get chilled. So I'll say goodbye."

"Give my regards to your other lover."

She turned on him, her eyes wide and dark and accusing. "Have those tests run again. I dare you."

"I don't need to."

"You'll wish you had," she promised him, eyes flashing. "One day you'll realize that I was telling you the truth, but it will be too late. And that will be the biggest irony of all. You'll have a child that you'll never know. You'll have denied the one thing in your life you profess to want the most!"

And she turned and walked away, oblivious to the tautness of his body, the harsh lines in his face. At that moment, she didn't care if she never saw him again.

Six

The confrontation worked on Bett's emotions like cold water. She went through the motions of living, but she felt nothing. Cul's words had cut like a knife. How could he be so blind? she wondered. How could he profess to care for her, and then refuse to believe her when she told him the truth?

Her appetite was the first casualty of the upset. David noticed that she wasn't eating and one night after the performance he took her out to an all-night eatery and tempted her with eggs and toast.

The timing was just right. She closed her eyes, savoring the smells, as outside the dark sky was pelting rain.

"Feel okay?" David asked softly, smiling at her from the stool next to hers at the deserted counter.

"Just fine, now," she agreed, digging heartily into the eggs. "I hadn't even realized I was hungry."

He chuckled, finishing off his toast. "It was a good night, though, wasn't it? We must be doing something right, the crowds are still pouring in."

"I almost blew it when I tripped, though." She groaned. "That stupid long gown does it to me every time. Thanks for catching me."

"My pleasure. I suppose they thought it was part of the act," he added dryly. "Nobody laughed."

"It isn't that kind of play." She sipped her coffee and her eyes were bitter. "I suppose Cul's gone back down to the Bahamas to see his playmate. Did you notice her at opening night? A knockout. Very uptown."

"No. I was too busy with my own few admirers," he replied. He leaned forward, pinning her with a dark, steady gaze. "Marry me, Bett," he said unexpectedly. "We'll raise the baby together."

She drew in a steadying breath and put down her fork slowly. "David, I can't," she told him sadly. "You're my friend, and I'm very fond of you. But I don't feel that way. I'm a one-man woman, despite the fact that the man in question is a solid-gold jackass who's totally blind."

"I won't ask for much," he persisted.

"You wouldn't get much, is the thing." She traced patterns in the icy fog on her glass of Coca-Cola. "No. Thank you, but no. It's my problem."

"It's everybody's problem," he argued. "Janet is worried about you, too. She's afraid for you, being in that apartment alone."

"Why?" she laughed. " I have good neighbors."

"You don't even know their names!"

"I know Mr. Bartholomew," she argued. "He's the gentleman who sings off-key. He looks like that big opera star, but he's not quite so generously proportioned."

"Or so talented," he mused.

"Anyway, he's always around, watching, when I come in at night. He said I needed a papa, and since I didn't have one of my own, he'd have to do." Tears welled in her eyes. "Honest to goodness, David, people have been so kind to me...."

"Don't." He touched her hand lightly with his. "Bett, don't. Look, suppose I go and talk to him? Tell him how it is with us?"

"Do you think he'd believe you?" she asked bitterly. "He said he loved me, David, but he doesn't think the baby is his. That's his misfortune, because of all the things he's ever wanted in his life, a baby was first priority."

"Then why didn't he get married and have one?" David asked simply.

She couldn't tell him that. She shrugged. "I don't know. Maybe he doesn't like the idea of being obligated to stay with one woman." Her eyes clouded. "Heaven knows, he got tired of me pretty quick, didn't he?"

"Bett," he groaned. His fingers tightened.

"It's all right," she said tautly. "We live and learn. I just feel so stupid. So cheap."

"You're not cheap."

"Yes, I am," she moaned. "I didn't even put up a fight. Oh, David, my parents tried so hard to give me the kind of values that would last me all my life. I always thought I'd get married and have children, I never dreamed I'd throw it all away on an illusion. Look at me now. Pregnant and alone...and how am I going to tell my mother and father? They live in a small suburb of Atlanta, they're respected in the community, they're good church-going people.'' She hid her face in her hands. "How can I expect them to live with the disgrace?''

"Bett, listen to me,'' he said quickly. "We can get married. They'll never have to know. I can give the baby a name, at least.''

"But it wouldn't be fair to you, can't you see that?'' she asked miserably. "David, I don't love you! And committing two wrongs won't make a right!''

He sighed angrily. "God, are you stubborn!''

"No, I'm stupid,'' she returned, drying her eyes. "And this is no time for self-pity. I've got to pull myself together.''

He watched her impatiently. "How will you manage by yourself?'' he grumbled.

"I'm not by myself,'' she replied. "I have you and Janet to cry on.''

He smiled gently. "Yes, I suppose so. How long have you known Janet?''

"Forever,'' she told him. She reached for her milk and sipped it. "She and I started out in acting together. But she decided that security was better and got a job as an assistant fashion designer. She loves it, and she's very good at it.'' She grinned. "Someday she's going to be as famous as Halston and Bill Blass.''

"I'd like to see some of her work,'' he murmured.

"Interested in dresses, are you?'' she murmured back with a wicked grin.

He chuckled. "Only in what's in them, actually." He looked thoughtful. "But Janet looks pretty good, whatever she wears."

"Indeed she does," she agreed.

"Does she go with anyone?"

"No. She hates men."

"How interesting." He leaned back in his chair. "Why?"

"Ask her sometime." She checked her watch. "David, this was delicious, but it's late and tomorrow's going to be another long day. The matinee..."

"Yes, I know." He sighed and got up to pay the bill. "How are you going to hold up?"

She stood, too. "I'm tough," she assured him, smiling. "Besides, it isn't like work to me. It's great fun. And my doctor, your friend, said that as long as I got plenty of rest it won't hurt me to stay active. He thinks it might actually help when I deliver."

"Did he tell you what it's going to be?" he teased.

"I wouldn't let him if he knew," she said firmly. "I want it to be a surprise. Ready to go?"

"Whenever you are, lady."

The apartment was very quiet when David left. She paced around, more concerned for her parents than she was for herself. She hadn't even considered them until today. It would hurt her mother so much....

She hugged herself, wondering why she hadn't thought of the consequences when she and Cul were together. She'd been so much in love that she'd been dazed, irresponsible. But now she was paying for that lapse, and despite the fact that she wanted the baby and would love it desperately, her life was in a horrible mess. All because of the new wave of permissive living, she had joined the ranks.

Most of the girls she knew took sex casually. Living with a man these days was nothing so shocking in a city like New York. But Bett hadn't been that way. She'd been reserved and unyielding, she'd held onto her principles. Until Cul walked back into her life and her mind went haywire. Well, she'd had her fantasy fulfilled. And look where it had led her. Her friends never got pregnant, but wham, a few nights with Cul and she was pregnant.

The worst part of it was what he'd said about wanting to make the arrangement permanent until he found out she was pregnant. The idiot! The *idiot*! As much as he'd wanted to father a child—and now that he had, he wouldn't accept the fact of its parentage. He thought she'd betrayed him with David. And that was so ludicrous. As if she could have betrayed him with any man, even in her mind. Cul was the only man she'd ever loved, or wanted. And he always would be, despite the fact that, at the moment, she hated him passionately.

It was her own fault, anyway. She could have said no. She could have walked away. She could at least have tried not to give in to her wild passion for the playwright. But she hadn't. And now she was going to have to pay for it.

The monologue she used in the play came back at her full force, and she lifted her eyes. "Oh, Lord," she whispered, "if you love little babies, forgive me and show me what to do."

All at once the weariness washed over her and she went to bed. It was the first night since it all began that she slept.

By the end of the week, she was ready to go back to her accountant with the money for the taxes. He was apologetic, but there had been an error, made by his secretary. She needed to come up with several thousand more dollars. He named an amount, which would barely leave her enough to buy groceries and pay the rent for the next few months.

When she got back to the apartment, she was in tears. She sat down heavily, white-faced. From bad to worse, wasn't that how the saying went? She reached for her investment account checkbook and wrote the check. She had to pay it, so she might as well get it over with. She put it with the tax form the accountant had given her, tucked it in the accompanying envelope and put a stamp on it. So much for the expensive visits to the doctor. She'd have to find another way.

She made herself a cup of hot herb tea, then went downtown for her last scheduled checkup with her doctor. Although she hadn't been feeling up to par lately, it was almost the last straw when he diagnosed her as anemic, prescribed expensive prenatal vitamins and told her to schedule another visit.

She told him she couldn't afford all these things, but he in turn gave her a stern lecture about her health and the needs of her baby, the infant developing inside her womb. What could she do?

It was a week before David and Janet found out about her condition. They were horrified to learn that she was in such dire straits. Janet had kept pumping, with David's help, until they wormed it out of her.

"Oh, my God!" Janet burst out. "That's the living end! Bett, let me call your parents...."

"No!" Bett whispered, white-faced. "Janet, if you do, I'll never forgive you! I can't stand the thought of my poor mother worrying over me. Her heart is already bad."

"All right, don't get upset," Janet said quickly. She sat down beside her friend, frowning, and held Bett's hand tight. "But, darling, we have to do something."

"Why? I'm taking care of myself," she protested. "I just have to cut back a bit."

"You shouldn't have to, that's the thing," Janet ground out. "Cul could afford to keep you in silk and ermine!"

"Cul doesn't have any responsibility to me, or this baby," Bett said roughly, and felt it. "It's my fault it happened. I'll take care of myself. That's all," she added, glaring at both of them when they opened their mouths. "Now be good friends and shut up. How about some coffee?"

She'd thought they'd let it go at that. She should have known better. Janet wasn't the type to turn her back on a friend in need. She lost her temper and called Cul, and then, calmer and nervous, she confessed to Bett what she'd done.

Bett just stared at her. It was early morning, and Janet had brought her a Danish and a cup of coffee from the deli, and she was still in her old flannel gown when the shorter woman blurted out the confession.

She stood rigidly with the pastry in one hand and the steaming coffee in its white Styrofoam cup in the other, not moving. In the faded blue flannel gown, with her hair streaming red and gold down her shoulders and her dark eyes wide, she was the picture of despair.

"Please don't hate me," Janet pleaded softly, her face contorting. "I was so mad.... Bett, I just cried thinking of you here, like this, and that stupid man... Oh, my gosh, anybody who knows you would realize that you wouldn't go to bed with a man you didn't love. And there's never been a man for you except Cul. If he wasn't such a jackass, he'd realize it. He should help out!"

"He owes me nothing," she managed huskily. "Nothing, Janet. I don't even want to see him again, don't you know? He's hurt me too much. I can't bear the thought of him seeing me like this!"

Her proud voice broke, and Janet wanted to cry, too. She took the pastry and the coffee and set it down, and took the broken woman into her arms.

"Forgive me," she whispered tearfully. "I put my foot in it, didn't I?"

Bett drew in a shuddering breath and dabbed at her eyes with her sleeve. "It's all right. You care about me and I appreciate it." Her drowned eyes looked into Janet's. "How did you find him?"

"I called the studio in Hollywood," came the quiet confession. "I'm really sorry."

"He isn't coming here?" Bett asked fearfully.

Janet turned away. "I don't know, I didn't ask. I was too busy telling him what an s.o.b. he was. I just went crazy. You're my friend. I couldn't stand it anymore." She turned. "Are you going to marry David? He said he asked you."

She felt the uneasiness in that question and tilted her head. "No, I told him no," she murmured. "I don't love him, you see, although he's a fine man."

"For a starving actor," Janet agreed with a nervous laugh, avoiding her friend's eyes. "He's nobody's dream man."

"But he's kind," Bett defended. "And fun to be with. He may be famous someday."

"I wouldn't bet on it," the smaller woman said bitingly.

"You just hate men, that's your trouble. Why don't you meet David halfway? I thought you two were getting along very well. At least you're not trying to verbally skewer each other lately."

"He's stopped needling me so much."

"And vice versa," Bett agreed.

Janet cleared her throat. "These sweetrolls are getting cold, and so is the coffee," she said hastily, and picked hers up. She glanced back. "I really am sorry I called Cul, Bett."

"Don't dwell on it," Bett said. "Cul being Cul, he probably forgot it all the minute he put the phone down. He'd never come cross country to see about me. Not in a million years. This coffee isn't bad, is it?"

Janet didn't say anything. But she was remembering the shocked silence on the other end of the line when she'd told Cul about Bett's circumstances. She wasn't that sure he wouldn't come. But now, she was tormented by fear that she'd caused more trouble for her friend. And God knew, Bett had all the trouble she could handle as it was.

Seven

Bett wondered if she was ever going to feel like her old self again. The anemia had weakened her, so that every step was difficult. She was going on willpower alone, and she noticed that her understudy was being carefully rehearsed. Well, she reminded herself, the production had to go on, with or without its leading lady. But how was she going to survive without her salary, if something happened to keep her from working?

The next day she managed to get to rehearsal, but in the middle of it, she collapsed. David got her back to her apartment and reluctantly left her there.

"I shouldn't go." He hesitated, his hand on the doorknob.

"Don't be silly," she chided, curling up on the couch. "I can take care of myself. It was just a little fainting spell. I am pregnant, you know."

"So you are." He sighed. "Well, you can always call the theater if you need me, I guess."

She smiled at him. "I guess."

He returned the smile, barely. "Okay. I'll check on you late this afternoon."

"Honestly, David, I'm all right," she returned. "I can always call Janet."

"You could call either of us, if you just would," he grumbled. "You're too independent, darling."

"I'm used to taking care of myself. Besides, Mr. Bartholomew..."

"...is your acting daddy, and he'll come if you yell. Yes, I know," he agreed. "So take care of yourself."

"Junior and I will be fine, worrywart."

He laughed and went out, closing the door behind him. Bett relaxed into the soft cushions of the worn sofa with a sigh. Her eyes glanced down at her shoes, noticing their worn condition. One sole was half off. Well, she'd either have to get used to them or have them resoled. The days of replacing worn items of clothing were long past. She could no longer afford that luxury.

The thought made her sad, and she did something that she'd never have done in front of her friends. She broke down and began to cry. It all seemed so hopeless somehow. No matter how hard she tried, things only got worse.

She was drying her tears on the hem of her faded, second-hand striped maternity blouse when an impatient, angry knock sounded at the door.

David, she assumed with a smile as she got up to answer it. He was probably still frustrated at having to leave her.

"I told you, I'm all right..." she began as she threw the bolt and opened the door. And froze. Because it wasn't David. It was Cul, and he was furious.

Just what I need, Bett thought miserably, World War III. "Well, come in," she said shortly, and turned her back on him, leaving him to follow. "I don't need to ask why you're here. Janet has already confessed."

"Don't tell me you didn't ask her to call me," he scoffed. He looked taller than ever, bigger. His blond hair was ruffled, as if his hands had tangled it, and his green eyes were accusing in a face darkened with bad temper.

She tossed her hair back from her shoulders and glared at him. "Go ahead," she invited with a mocking smile and a graceful sweep of her hand. "Get it all out of your system."

He just stood there, breathing deeply, the pupils of his eyes so contracted that they seemed to be invisible. "I can't remember the last time I was this angry," he told her flatly. "You and I both know that child isn't mine, Bett. Involving other people isn't going to bring me around. It will only turn me against you. Nothing you say or do will convince me that you didn't take a lover on the side."

"I'd already figured that out, all by myself," she assured him. She folded her arms over her breasts and stared at him defiantly. "I want nothing from you. I never did. Janet and David were worried about me. Janet took it upon herself to enlist you. I didn't ask her to. I'd be happy if I never saw you again."

"If Hadison is so damned concerned, why won't he marry you?" he began the old argument.

She threw up her hands and turned toward the kitchen. "I can't argue with stone," she told the coffeepot as she filled it and started it perking.

"I didn't come here to argue. I came here to tell you that if you don't stop fingering me as the father of your child, I'll take you to court."

"That sounds like fun," she remarked absently. "I can see the headlines—ACTRESS IMPREGNATED BY TOILET SEAT..."

"Stop it! It's not funny!"

Probably not, she agreed silently, but it was either laugh or cry, and she'd had quite enough crying. "That's as good an explanation as yours," she replied, turning to face him. Behind her, the aging coffeepot began to make embarrassing noises as it heated up and started perking.

"You little idiot," he burst out, angrily, "don't you think I'd give blood to be responsible for your condition? I write plays about pregnant women, I dream about children... but facts are facts! Shall I give you my doctor's phone number and let you speak to him personally?" he added, visibly exasperated. "Maybe if you hear it from him, you'll realize how hopeless this accusation really is!"

She searched his craggy face quietly. He was aging. There were lines of strain all around his chiseled mouth, his long, elegant nose, his deep-set eyes. He looked as if he hadn't slept well in a long time, as if he'd been worrying. Well, that was pretty common. Perhaps one of his girls was giving him hell. The thought depressed her even more.

"You'd make a great trial lawyer," she murmured absently. "All that single-minded determination is wasted on theater."

"Are you listening to me?" he challenged.

"Of course I am, Cul. I'm listening to you calling me a liar. You are," she asserted when he started to interrupt. "You're saying that I was two-timing you. Which only goes to prove that you don't know me at all. I was so besotted with you that I couldn't have let another man touch me. So how do you explain my faceless lover?"

He shrugged uncomfortably. "Perhaps you drank a little too much at a party...."

She threw up her hands. "Perhaps I was kidnapped by a flying saucer and seduced by aliens!"

"Can't you ever be serious?" he flared, shifting again.

"I don't dare," she told him solemnly. "If I let myself think about what you're saying, I'll have hysterics and Mr. Bartholomew will come running up those stairs and kill you!" She blinked. "There's a thought."

"Bartholomew?" His eyes narrowed. "Does he come up here to see you often?"

"That's the spirit, Cul, just keep tossing out accusations. Why stop with Mr. Bartholomew?" she continued heatedly. "Why not add the postman, the grocery boy, the bus driver, and the man who sells hot dogs on the corner? My God, I'm a prostitute! I created my own red light district...!"

"Stop it," he ground out.

"You keep saying that." She sighed wearily and turned back to the coffeepot, taking down a cup from

the cupboard to fill with the watery dark liquid. She
had to make it half strength—not only because of the
caffeine, but because she couldn't afford to buy much
coffee. The cup was chipped and had a hairline crack
down its off-white surface, but like her shoes, it
couldn't be replaced, either. With a sigh, she filled her
cup. She was having to pinch pennies until they
screamed, for the baby's sake.

Boy, she thought, has this baby got a stupid father.
She patted the little rounded mound and smiled at it.
That's okay, kid, she thought, you and I will make it
somehow.

He came up behind her. "Have you got an extra
cup?" he asked hesitantly.

"Sure. Where would you like it?" She turned,
finding him much too close. She backed away a little.
"I can think of a perfect place."

"My insurance doesn't cover that," he murmured
dryly, and a faint smile touched his hard mouth.

"The cups are up there," she gestured vaguely,
turning back to the worn sofa with her own hot cup.

She heard the cupboards open and close. There was
a long silence before she heard coffee being poured
into a cup. He opened the refrigerator and there was
an even longer pause. It wasn't until she heard the
rough sigh that she realized what he was thinking. All
she had in the way of groceries were milk and cheese,
courtesy of a special nutrition program for pregnant
women, a few slices of bread and some canned soup,
with only a few staples. She was going to the store tomorrow to stock up again. But she knew exactly what
he was thinking when she got a look at his face.

"I'm not going to starve," she said, putting on a magnificent front. "Tomorrow is grocery day."

His eyes went over her as he cradled the cup in his hands. "Nutrition is important," he began. "Especially in the first few months!"

"No!" she exclaimed. "Why didn't my obstretrician tell me?"

"When you visit him, that is? Janet said you'd cut your visits to the bone."

"My life is none of your business," she told him.

"Do your parents know?"

Her face went pasty white. She clenched her teeth and stared down into the cup in her lap. "No."

"Oh, boy," he whistled through his teeth. He sat down beside her. "I thought you'd have told them."

"My parents aren't the kind of people who have unwed mothers for daughters," she said sadly. "My mother has a heart condition, and any kind of shock could kill her. They're deeply religious people, Cul. They raised me in the church."

"All right, then, I'll take care of you," he said, as if the thought of it galled him to the back teeth.

Her head lifted, and her eyes scorched him. She shook her head. "No way, honey. I'd take help from an armed robber before I'd take it from you."

"You can't live like this," he began.

"Other people do. I'll make out. You just mind your own complicated love life, sweet man, and Junior and I will take care of each other. When he's old enough," she amended.

He stared at her stomach again and dragged his eyes away. "You need food."

"I'm not starving," she grumbled. "I'm just careful. I wouldn't endanger the baby for the world. But I can't have everything—I'm just cutting back a little."

"You shouldn't have to!" he shot at her. He glared down at the coffee cup. "The baby's father should be looking after you."

"Why?" she asked reasonably. "It's my baby."

"You didn't make it all by yourself."

"Like hell I didn't," she replied hotly. "According to you, that's exactly how it happened!"

He got up, livid with controlled fury. He stared down at her violently for an instant before he drained his cup and put it on the coffee table.

"This isn't getting us anywhere," he said after a minute. "I'd better go."

"What a lovely idea." She batted her long eyelashes up at him. "Do give my love to Mary or Kate or Gail or Beverly or whoever you're sleeping with these days."

That made him even madder, but he managed not to answer back. "Goodnight," he said as he turned to go.

"I'll see to it that Janet never bothers you again," she called after him. "Even if I have to gag her."

The door slammed furiously behind him. And with that angry face out of sight, all her borrowed composure vanished. She caught her breath slowly, grateful that she'd been able to keep him from seeing how helpless she really was. Now he wouldn't believe what Janet had told him. He'd go away and leave her alone, and she could try to find some peace.

The man standing outside her apartment building in the rain was unaware of her vulnerabilities. He was letting the misty wetness collect around his blond hair, on his gray suit, without even feeling it. Why wouldn't she admit the truth? Why was she trying to make him feel responsible for her pregnancy? Didn't she know what it was doing to him?

He walked down the sidewalk, merging with the crowds, feeling alone and vaguely helpless. Her words haunted him. She'd said that she was too besotted with him to have another lover, and it made sense. That was why it was so terrible, because it was logical. He'd never have believed she could go from him to another man. He couldn't accept that. But . . .

Yes, he thought. But . . .

His doctor had been so certain. He strained, trying to remember the exact words. Highly unlikely, the man had said. It was highly unlikely that he would ever father a child. His eyes narrowed. That meant . . . it could be possible.

But as soon as the thought came, he dismissed it. Bett was playing games with him. She was paying him back for walking out on her, and nothing more. Perhaps she wasn't even as far along as she'd made out, perhaps it had happened soon after he'd left for Hollywood.

He had himself almost convinced. Until he remembered that only three weeks had transpired from his departure to her pregnancy. And that roundness, that mound of her belly, was real. It hadn't happened in his absence. It had to have happened while they were lovers. And that hurt most of all.

He found himself at the corner grocery, gathering up food in a basket. Well, she had to eat. Whoever the child belonged to, he couldn't very well let it starve. He allowed himself to wonder if it would be a boy or a girl. He smiled softly, thinking about Bett's unusual coloring, her reddish-gold hair and dark eyes and pale complexion with just a scattering of freckles over the bridge of her pretty nose. He sighed. A little girl like that would be beautiful. She'd wear frilly dresses and little boys would follow her around, and one day she'd start dating and big boys would follow her around. His face hardened. He'd kill any boy who messed around with his little girl! Of course, he reminded himself, it wouldn't be his little girl. . . .

"I said, is that all, sir?" the grocery boy asked a second time, as politely as he could. The man looked like a potential homicidal maniac.

"What?" Cul cleared his throat. He hadn't even realized that he was being checked out. "Oh, yes, that's all, thanks." He produced his wallet with a sheepish grin and paid the boy.

All the way back to Bett's apartment, he was thinking about the baby. It wouldn't hurt him to take care of her. He could well afford it. He wanted a baby so much, he wanted something to love and spoil. Love was the one commodity that had been lacking in his own life. He'd never known much about his parents, having spent most of his young life in an exclusive boarding school. His parents hadn't really wanted him. Eventually there had been a girl that he'd wanted to marry. They'd had routine tests, and he'd volunteered for the fertility test, to be sure that he could produce children. And that was when he'd received the shock of his life. He barely even remembered the girl. He'd concocted some story about why they couldn't marry, and walked out, leaving her in tears. And since that day, he'd avoided any kind of entanglement. Until now. Until Bett. All the hard work, all the stubborn pride in the world hadn't saved him from her. He couldn't stop caring, even while believing she'd been with some other man behind his back.

He knocked at the door of her apartment with the groceries in one big arm, and waited impatiently for her to open it.

Bett heard the knock and would have ignored it, except that she couldn't be sure it wasn't David or Janet.

Grumbling, she opened the door, and found Cul there. Again.

"Go away," she said.

"Not until I've put these in the kitchen," he said shortly. "And don't you dare say another word. You said earlier you could sink your damned pride for the baby's sake. Okay, doll, let's see you do that, right now."

She tried to think of a comeback while he went to the cabinet and began putting away groceries. "I don't want anything from you," she said curtly.

"Then throw it out the window," he replied carelessly.

He put canned goods in the cabinets and blocks of cheese and fresh meats and milk into the refrigerator, along with fresh fruit that made Bett's mouth water. There was even lettuce and the French bread she loved so much. Tears came to her eyes but she quickly dashed them away. Imagine, getting teary over lettuce!

"I don't need your charity," she tried again.

"You need something, honey," he told her. He folded the grocery bag and stuck it under the sink. "This is worse than the apartment I had in Atlanta, all those years ago."

"You never needed to live like that," she replied, folding her arms over the colorful striped smock. "You had money, even then. Tons of it."

"Yes, but not my own," he said. He put a new bag of coffee by the pot and poured himself another cup of the hot liquid, offering to do the same for her, but she refused. "I like earning what I get, all by myself."

She drew in a deep breath and averted her eyes. "Thanks for the groceries," she said. "I'll pay you back when I'm solvent."

"Did I ask you to pay me back?"

"I will, nevertheless," she returned, staring at him with all the hauteur she could muster.

He smiled at the pose. "Are you sure you aren't the reincarnation of Elizabeth the First? You do look the image of her portraits."

"I could hardly qualify for her reputation, these days," she reminded him with a sigh. She went to the window and looked down at the busy street with the haze of rain making everything gray. "It looks dreary out there."

"It is. I hear your understudy is being rehearsed overtime."

That was a sore spot, but she faced it without flinching. "Yes, she has," she replied quietly. "And after this morning, I may be replaced by her." It really bothered her, putting that fear into words. If she was replaced, and she could understand that the show had to go on, how would she manage? She stared at the floor. "I'm having some problems with anemia."

"Are you having treatment?" he asked, sounding concerned.

"I'm all right," she said.

"Medicine costs money."

She paled, glancing at him.

"So I thought. I'll take care of the cost."

"You will not," she replied coldly. "Over my dead body!"

"It might be that, if you don't start taking care of yourself. And to make sure that you do," he added, pursing his lips as he studied her, "I've decided to marry you."

Eight

—

Marriage? Had she heard him right? She gaped at him, her dark eyes wide and unbelieving.

"No comment, Bett?" he asked mildly. "I meant it, if that's why you're staring at me in shock."

She could hardly believe that. Certainly she couldn't fool herself into thinking it was passionate love of her. He'd said that he cared deeply, but men were emotional creatures in the depths of an affair. And if he'd truly loved her, he'd have believed the child was his, even over the stated opinion of a respected physician. It was pity that prompted the proposal, that was obvious.

"Thank you," she said after a minute, resuming her seat on the sofa. "But I won't marry you, Cul."

He started to speak, paused long enough to sit back down beside her, and tried again. "You need financial help, you must realize that. For God's sake, you can't support yourself like this, let alone yourself and a baby. There are going to be medical expenses, perhaps large ones. You'll need baby things, more visits to the doctor, excellent nutrition . . ."

"I'm aware of that," she said tautly.

"Unless you tell your parents, there's no way you can manage," he said curtly, "and you know it. Hadison and Janet can't help, they have enough problems of their own. The only person left is me."

"I'm not your problem," she said, lifting her chin.

"You keep claiming that you are," he replied. "Are you admitting that it isn't my child?"

She got up. "Let me walk you to the door, Cul, dear. I'm sure you must have someone waiting for you."

"Think about it," he said as he rose, towering over her. "I don't mind marrying you."

"But I mind marrying you, you see," she said as calmly as she could. "What you're offering me is charity. As I've said before, there are agencies for that. Thanks all the same, but my baby and I will manage very well by ourselves."

He frowned. He hadn't expected that reaction.

"Puzzled, darling?" she laughed as she opened the front door for him. "It's very simple, really. I can't go through life with a man who doesn't trust me. That's no kind of relationship at all. I'd rather struggle along by myself."

"We've gone over this until I'm sick of it," he shot back. "Why can't you just tell the truth?"

"Ironically enough, I have," she replied. "But you seem to be deaf as well as blind. Goodbye, Cul. It was nice seeing you again."

"Dick Hamilton will have to let you go," he said under his breath. "Don't you realize that we've all got a hell of a bundle tied up in this production? We can't carry you on and off stage every night and during matinees!"

"Then Dick can tell me so," she replied, even though she knew it was the truth. "He's the stage manager after all. Your part in the play is over."

He glared at her. "I'm not through."

"You are for tonight," she replied. "Good night. I'm very tired. Junior needs his rest."

He sighed wearily, letting his eyes run down her body. "Oh, hell," he muttered.

"And don't curse at me," she flashed back. "You were the one who insisted that I didn't need to take precautions! If it's anyone's fault that I got this way, it's yours!"

"I'm sterile, damn you. Sterile!"

She stared down at her belly and back up at him. "Sure you are." And she closed the door firmly in his face and locked it.

David came back that evening on his way to supper and he looked uncomfortable.

"Dick's coming over first thing in the morning to talk to you," he said reluctantly.

"And I know what about," she said with a wan smile. "Tell him it's not necessary. I understand, and I won't hold grudges. I really don't feel like working."

"Why won't you marry me?" he groaned. "I'll take care of you!"

Bett wondered absently if the *Guiness Book of World Records* had anyone else who could claim two proposals in less than two hours. "David, we'd starve together," she said. "I love you, but not that way. You're my nice big brother. Besides, Janet would never forgive me if I married her favorite sparring partner."

He glowered at her. "Janet doesn't know I'm alive."

"Take her out and feed her. Women's eyesight improves marvelously when they're fed," she suggested.

He thought about that. "I suppose we could discuss what we're going to do about you," he agreed, giving her an appraising look.

"That sounds ominous, like I'm bad cheese that needs to be disposed of," she said, laughing.

"Mr. Bartholomew met me at the staircase," he mentioned. "He said you'd had a visitor."

"Cul," she affirmed darkly. "And you tell our mutual friend Janet to please forget his telephone number."

"Did he upset you?" he asked, as if he meant to go out and pound Cul to a pulp. That would have been interesting to watch, considering that David was half Cul's size and temperament.

"He offered to marry me," she said.

He gaped. "Well?"

"I said no," she told him.

"Idiot! It would have solved all your problems!"

"It would have created more," she said flatly. She leaned back against the sofa, feeling vaguely nau-

seated and frankly tired. "He still won't believe it's his
child. How can I marry a man who only offers out of
misplaced pity? No, thanks. Things are bad enough
already." She looked around her. "I guess I'll have to
go and live at the women's mission. . . ."

"No!" He was horrified.

"Don't worry, I was just kidding. There are Chris-
tian homes for people like me. I'll find something."

David stood up, looking formidable. "I'll kill him."

"Too easy," she replied. Her eyes closed. "I just
need some rest, I'll think up something in the morning. There's bound to be something I'm able to do,
you know."

He looked more concerned than ever. "Well, get
some sleep. Janet and I will see what we can come up
with. Dick's really sorry about it."

"I'm an actress," she reminded him. "I understand."

"You know what a marshmallow he is under all the
gruffness. He's sick about it."

So was she, but she put on her bravest smile and reassured David that she was going to be fine. But when
he left, the gloom seemed to settle over everything.
Things had never looked so utterly hopeless.

It was almost midnight when Janet and David came
by the apartment. Janet looked flushed and happy and
David looked stunned. There were definite undercur-
rents, but Bett pretended not to notice. She curled up
on the sofa in her faded green bathrobe and listened
to Janet's excited offer.

"One of my clients, Lovewear, is bringing out a line
of maternity clothes," Janet said enthusiastically.
"But they'd like to have a really pregnant woman

model them. If you think you could do it, I could tell them for you and lay some groundwork.''

Bett only smiled. Her bubbly friend couldn't begin to understand the complications of mingled pregnancy and anemia.

"Dear friend," she said gently, "I love you. But if I can't stand on stage to act, I certainly can't stand to model."

Janet let out a sigh. "No. I forgot. I guess I take it so for granted that I don't realize how tiring it is. And in your condition . . . I just wanted to help.''

"And you have. By caring about me. Want some coffee?" she offered.

"No," David answered for her. He caught Janet's hand and pulled her up with him, his eyes lingering for a minute longer than necessary on her upturned face. "We, uh, have someplace to go."

"Yes," Janet faltered. She shifted restlessly, firing a nervous glance at Bett.

Bett grinned. "Have fun."

Janet visibly relaxed. On a nonverbal level, she'd asked if Bett minded that she was getting involved with David, and Bett had reassured her, all without a single word being spoken. And without dear David even realizing what was going on around him.

"I'll call you tomorrow," Janet promised.

"We will," David amended with a grin. "Get some sleep, Bett."

"Sure. Bye."

She locked the door behind them. Well, at least someone's life was getting better. She was delighted that her two best friends were finding they had more in common than just Bett.

As expected, Dick Hamilton turned up early the following morning. But he came with an unexpected proposition.

"The production company is going to absorb your medical bills," Dick told her with a grin. "And we're going to let you continue, with the understanding that if you feel you can't keep up the pace, you let your understudy take over for you, as she did last night."

She could have bawled. "Oh, Dick, but I can't let you..."

"It was my idea," he said firmly, watching her face. "You're so good in that role that no one can replace you without forcing us to close down. The public pays to see you, and only you. So we're going to make sure you have the best medical care available, even a doctor on the set if you need one. How about it?"

She laughed softly. "You can't imagine how worried I was..."

"I think I have a pretty good idea. Get some rest. But first, call the doctor and make an appointment."

"I can go on tonight," she said, smiling. "I'm much better, really. I've got all kinds of food in the refrigerator and I've been eating," she confessed sheepishly. She bit her lip as she realized what she was rerevealing. Probably he knew that Cul had brought her some badly needed groceries. With her medical expenses covered, she could afford to feed herself properly.

"We think of you as an investment, you know," Dick told her before he left. "A very nice one, and you're paying off better than you know. But besides all that, we care about you. I wish I'd known sooner that you were pinching pennies. I'd have done something about it."

"I didn't want to bother anyone," she said.

He shook his head. "Women!" He threw up his hands. "See you later, kid."

She felt a new energy flowing through her in the days that followed. The expensive prenatal vitamins her obstetrician had prescribed, along with her new and more than adequate diet, got her back to work and on the road to recovery. What a stroke of luck, she thought, that the production people had decided to subsidize her. She almost suspected Cul, but she was sure her attitude had convinced him to give up trying to help her.

At least, until a week had gone by. Late one afternoon he showed up at her door with a huge box under one arm while she was resting.

"You look better," he said, studying her in the faded green bathrobe she was wearing over a long cotton gown.

She put a slender hand to her tangled hair and moved it away from her face. "I feel better, thanks."

He came inside, wearing jeans and a pullover shirt that was as green as his eyes. "I brought you something." He held the box out to her.

She eyed him suspiciously. "Why are you bringing me presents?"

"It's from the whole production company," he said, shrugging. "Dick's idea," he added, watching her through narrowed eyes so that he caught the faint gleam of disappointment in her dark eyes before they lowered to the box.

She opened it and found three maternity outfits inside, all very chic and pretty and just her size. She held up a cream and beige one, a skirt and overblouse combination with a jabot collar. "It's lovely," she said breathlessly, and laughed. "Oh, how sweet of them! You know, I've been buying my things from yard sales...."

His face went hard and he turned away, his hands jammed deep in the pockets of his jeans. "We thought you might like something new to wear."

She glanced at his rigid back. "Would you like some coffee?" she asked.

"I'll make it," he murmured gruffly. "Your idea of coffee is hot water with a drop of brown food color in it."

"Coffee is expensive!" she shot at him.

He whirled. "Then I'll buy it for you!" he rejoined. "God, you exasperate me! It's a fight all the way to do anything for you."

"I'm proud," she replied coldly. "I don't want charity from you. I don't want anything from you!"

"Not even the baby you're carrying?" he asked quietly.

"It isn't yours, remember?" she asked, her smile plainly malicious. "You said so."

She looked cold. All the lovely color had drained from her face, the bright joy of the gifts siphoned off like water from a silver bowl.

"I'm sorry," he apologized, his deep voice echoing around the room. "I didn't come to upset you."

That was new. Cul never apologized. Perhaps one of his women was busy reforming him.

She sat down on the arm of the sofa and touched her pretty new things, smiling softly. "I can wear one of these to church on Sunday," she remarked absently.

"I didn't know you went."

"I didn't used to," she agreed. "Mr. Batholomew decided that it might help my outlook, so he bundled me up one Sunday and took me with him."

He glared at her. "I don't like that."

She glared back. "I can go to church if I want!"

His eyes glittered at her as he turned from the coffeepot he'd filled and started perking. "If you want to go to church, I'll take you."

Her eyebrows lifted. "You wouldn't know what the inside of a church looked like."

"So I'll find out," he returned. "That off-key baritone has no business hanging around you!"

"Suppose it's his baby?" she asked sweetly.

He ran a furious hand through his thick blond hair. "Give me strength," he muttered. "Of course it's not his baby!"

She clicked her tongue and folded her arms over her breasts. "You're narrowing down the possibilities," she said disapprovingly. "Before long, you'll run out of possible fathers. Just think what an exciting christening it's going to be," she mused, smiling. "David and Mr. Bartholomew, the hot dog man, the mailman..."

He moved toward her with eyes that blazed, and before she could retreat, he had her up in his hard arms. Amazing, she thought through her apprehension, how strong he was.

"I could..." he said through his teeth.

"You could what?" she asked, staring up at him.

His expression wavered between words and actions. "Elisabet," he said in a voice husky with strain and frustration. And then his mouth covered hers.

She wanted to struggle, but she was afraid she might make him drop her, and that wouldn't be good for the child he didn't think he'd fathered. So she let him kiss her, lying acquiescent in his strong arms while his mouth took a slow, fierce toll of her soft lips.

"This won't solve anything, Cul," she whispered into his mouth as it lifted just slightly to catch a breath.

"It might stop the ache," he whispered back. His cheek nuzzled hers as he dropped down onto the sofa with Bett across his lap.

"Don't you have enough women to do that?" she asked accusingly.

He looked down into her dark, quiet eyes and smiled. "I'd say there's a lack of trust on your part as well as mine, wouldn't you?" His hand slid from her cheek to her shoulder and lifted, to follow the path of his eyes to the slight swell of her stomach. He touched her there and she stiffened.

"No, don't fight me," he said, his voice quiet, almost tender. "I don't have to tell you how I feel about pregnancy. All my adult life, I've wanted a child of my own. But I've never touched a pregnant woman. I've never seen one, not close, like this. I want to know everything." His eyes watched his hand moving, and he talked as if he were talking to himself. "I want to know everything about it. How it feels, how it looks. I want to know the changes it makes."

"You could go to medical school," she suggested with her last vestige of protective humor. The sound of his voice, the seductive touch of his tanned fingers was robbing her of her defenses.

His hand spread, covering the firm mound, warm and oddly protective. "How does it feel?" he asked, lifting his eyes back to hers.

"I'm sick most of the time." She averted her eyes to his broad chest, to its quick rise and fall under the soft knit of his green shirt. "I tire easily. It's hard to stay awake at night. I'm very sore in certain places."

"Where?"

She touched her breasts. "They swell. And there's the heartburn . . . I think it's the worst of all."

"How does it feel?" he persisted, stressing the word as he searched her eyes.

"Marvelous, darling," she breathed. "The most awesome experience I've ever had. In a few months, he'll begin to move, and then he'll be born, and I can hold him, touch him. I won't be alone anymore, ever. I'll belong to someone. I'll have someone who belongs to me." She sighed quietly and smiled. "You don't understand that, do you, Cul? Belonging, I mean. You've never really wanted that kind of closeness and commitment. You've been single all your life, and you like it."

"I want a family," he returned curtly.

"No," she argued. "I don't think you really do. I think you like believing that bull about being sterile. Because it protects you from getting involved. It's your security."

"You're out of your mind," he said, his voice cutting. He stood up, moving away to light a cigarette.

Funny, she thought, watching, she hadn't seen him smoke in a long time.

"Am I?" she demanded, standing. "I've hit on it, haven't I? Your terrible secret. You can't let yourself admit that this is your baby, because then all the walls would come down around you. You'd have to prove that you really wanted that family you claim you covet, the security of marriage. And you couldn't, could you? It would involve something you know nothing about—giving!"

"I'm no miser," he began, facing her.

"Emotionally, you are," she corrected. She linked her hands behind her to study his rigid figure. He had a perfect physique, she thought dreamily, and had to mentally shake herself to get back to reality. "No caring man could have done to me what you did in Atlanta," she said. "You humiliated me in front of the whole cast, and you knew you were doing it. You said it was to save me from a childless relationship with no hope of marriage, but that wasn't really true. It was to save yourself."

He sighed roughly. "No."

"Yes, darling. Even when we started getting involved here, you fought it every step of the way. It was desire that propelled you into my bed, Cul, not undying love and devotion. I mistook it for that. But one phone call to California gave me the proof of your devotion. Cherrie, wasn't it . . . ?"

"She was just another girl," he murmured. "And we didn't . . ."

"Didn't you?" she asked, her eyes unbelieving. "I called to tell you I was pregnant, and you went through the roof. It wasn't yours, you were sure. Even though you knew," she stressed fiercely, "that I was too much in love with you to let another man make love to me. You knew that! But you gave me hell for accusing you of being my child's father."

"I'm not," he said huskily.

"Poor Cul." She shook her head. "You've grown so accustomed to your own company that you don't want any intruders in your life. You won't trust anyone enough to love them. Or be loved by them. You say you want a child, but you don't. You don't want anyone, Cul. Because love demands unselfishness and blind trust—two qualities you simply don't possess."

"That's not true," he replied, and his voice was icy cold. "I'd give anything for a child of my own, for a wife and a home."

"Of course you would," she agreed, humoring him. She walked to her front door and opened it. This, she thought, was getting to be a habit. "That's why you have an unending supply of groupies in your life, and hot and cold running women in your apartment."

He was glaring at her, his cigarette firing up curls of smoke, his eyes frankly unpleasant.

"Think what you like," he told her.

"Thanks for your permission. Good night, Cul."

"It isn't night."

"Don't clutter up my life with a lot of irrelevant facts. Please leave, I'm having an orgy this afternoon, and I have to peel two pounds of grapes."

Once he would have laughed at that, but his face was rigid and cold. The real man, under the veneer that he'd worn for so long. He stared at her and for a instant he did hate her, because she'd shown him a side of his own personality that he didn't want to see.

There was some truth in her accusation, but he wasn't ready for it.

"If I walk out that door, I won't come back," he warned quietly. "I'll ask you once more to marry me. Only once."

"I don't want to marry you," she said. "You may see yourself as the perfect mate. You're rich and sexy and great in bed and you have an impeccable family tree. But I wouldn't fit in that august company, you see. I want a down-to-earth man who loves me. As husband material, honey, Mr. Bartholomew has aces up on you. He has a heart as big as all outdoors, even if his singing voice does sound like a dull saw on tin."

"Then marry the sweet old gentleman," Cul told her as he walked through the open door, "and to hell with him, for all I care!"

"Don't trip on your ego, big man!" she threw after his retreating figure, and slammed the door so hard that a picture fell off the wall.

After the temper, of course, came tears. She sat down and did what she'd done most in past days. She bawled. Damn men everywhere, and Edward Mc-Cullough most of all! She hoped she never saw him again in her whole life!

Nine

Bett worried about what she'd said to Cul, despite her anger toward him. Like her, he used cynicism for a shield to keep people from hurting him. But she'd hit home. He was afraid of the responsibility of loving, and that was why he ran from commitment. Perhaps he'd never known much love in his early life. She knew very little about that part of him; it was something he'd never liked to discuss.

Although her heart was breaking, pride kept her going on stage. She couldn't let the production company down. She put every spare shred of emotion into her characterization, and she was proud of the reviews that raved about the revival of Cul's excellent play.

Cul might have vanished into thin air after that
night he came to her apartment. No one saw him or
heard from him. Bett was almost certain he was back
out in California, working on the screenplay that he
hadn't quite finished, but she'd stopped listening to
conversations that included him. He was no longer a
part of her life. Now there was only the baby to think
about. Only her child.

Thanks to the increased medical care she was getting because of the company's generosity, she was
feeling better by the day. She had more energy. The
anemia was under control. She was enjoying the role
she played more and more. The only thing missing
from her life was the man she loved. Cul would probably never forgive her for what she'd said to him. On
the other hand, it would take her a long time to forgive the things he'd accused her of. And, especially,
for denying the child that could only be his.

Three long, lonely weeks passed before Bett found
out that Cul was still in town.

"Dick went to see Cul last night," Janet remarked
one evening after the performance, while Bett re-
moved her heavy stage makeup in her dressing room.

Bett's heart leaped, but she didn't let her excitement show. "Did he?"

"Apparently he's decided to work himself to
death," Janet said on a cold laugh. Cul wasn't one of
her favorite people, not after the way he'd treated Bett.
"He's locked up tight in his apartment, and not even
eating some nights. Dick told David that Cul threw out
everything he'd been working on and has started the
new screenplay from scratch. He had a set deadline, so
that meant he had to double up on time to make it."

Bett couldn't help but wonder if Cul's feverish schedule had anything to do with what she'd said to him. Her conscience twinged a little. She knew from past experience that he was capable of pushing himself all too hard on deadlines. He'd go for days without eating or sleeping, he'd literally work himself into exhaustion.

"Surely you aren't feeling sorry for him?" Janet demanded. "Not after what he's done to you?"

"Of course I'm not feeling sorry for him," Bett said defensively. She brushed her hair briskly but her troubled eyes met Janet's in the mirror.

"You and your conscience," Janet chided softly, smiling. "It's going to be your undoing someday. Cul isn't your responsibility."

"I suppose not."

"Anyway, it's just work," Janet persisted stubbornly. "Just work, not anything to do with you, and you know it."

But Janet didn't know about that last, bitter argument. She didn't know that Bett had hurt him.

It was too late to do anything that night, but the next day she cornered Dick long enough to ask him what was going on with Cul.

"Honest to God, I don't know," he admitted, jamming his hands into his pockets. "I've seen him overwork himself before, but nothing like this. The last time I saw him, he was as pasty as cornmeal, and about as coherent. If he's writing in that condition, it must be pure gibberish. He won't eat. He's drinking."

"Cul?" She was shocked. She'd never seen him take more than a social drink, and he was reluctant to do that. He'd mentioned once that watching his father toss it back at cocktail parties had cured him.

"It doesn't sound like him, does it?" he mused. "Well, there's nothing I can do. I mentioned that it might be an idea if he got out of his apartment for a while, and he told me . . . well, the gist of it was to get out and leave him alone. I have excellent survival instincts. I won't go back unless I'm asked."

"Was he sick?" Bett asked gently, her eyes wide and soft with helpless concern.

"Yes, I think he was, Bett," Dick told her reluctantly. "How sick, I don't know. Perhaps that was the reason for the booze. It's supposed to kill germs, isn't it?"

Despite Janet's assertion that Cul's health was none of Bett's business, and over all her own genuine misgivings, she still felt guilty about what Dick had told her. Cul was the father of her child. Could she, in all good conscience, allow him to work himself to death?

No, she thought. There had been some good times. For the sake of those, and the baby, she had to do something for him.

She swallowed her pride and went to his apartment the next evening she had off, trying not to remember better days and happier visits here. Well, apparently he was willing to see her, at least, because when she buzzed his apartment, he let her into the building. But it took five minutes to get him to the door after she got upstairs.

The man who faced her across the threshold looked as if he'd been raised from the dead. He was thinner. His unshaven face had a whitish tint, and his green eyes were bloodshot. His hair looked more brown than blond and had lost its bright gleam. He was half in, half out of an expensive Cardin bathrobe and he looked terrible.

"Bett?" he asked, dazed.

"The very same," she agreed. "Oh, Mr. McCullough, how you have changed."

His chin lifted pugnaciously and he glared at her, swaying a little on his bare feet. "What do you want? Have you come to give me another character reading? Well, no thanks, lady, one was enough!"

"Don't growl, you'll upset the baby," she said calmly, easing past him into the apartment. It would have given a veteran cleaning woman heart failure. Bett had never seen such a mess. Full ashtrays, dirty plates and glasses everywhere, clothes strewn from one visible corner to another, wads of paper here and there, even a couple of typewriter ribbons unwound on the carpet.

"Go away," Cul said shortly, glaring at her from the door, which he was holding open.

She stripped off the long beige sweater coat she'd found at a close-out sale, disclosing her pretty yellow maternity dress with its short puffy sleeves. It felt like spring, even though it would be a few more weeks until warm weather actually came. "Shut up, darling," she said carelessly, shaking her head as she stared around at the disarray. "Why don't you take a shower and I'll make you something to eat."

"There's no food," he muttered.

"Then I'll go and get some. Go on." She went past him to close the door and started to push him toward the bedroom.

"Now, look here, Bett," he began, stopping in his tracks.

"You look here, or you'll fall over your big feet. Shower first, then food."

He started to speak, threw up his hands, and wobbled into his bedroom, slamming the door behind him.

Bett went to the kitchen and opened the refrigerator. She quickly closed it again. The shopping could wait until she made something to eat and washed some dishes to serve it in. The freezer boasted a steak, a big juicy one, so she cooked that and opened a can of English peas and creamed them. There was a packet of creamed corn in the freezer, so she boiled that and added it to the sparse menu. She cleaned all the dishes lining the sink and filled a plate.

By the time she knocked on Cul's bedroom door, she'd even made a dent in the cluttered living room.

"Well?" he demanded as she opened the door.

"Much better." she said approvingly. He'd changed into blue silk pajamas. His hair was clean and blond again, although he still had a sickly look. "I'll bring your supper."

"There's nothing in there that's fit to eat," he protested.

She ignored him, returning to the kitchen to put his plate and a cup of black coffee on a tray. She tucked it over his lap on his king-sized bed, and sat down in a chair with her own black coffee to watch him eat.

He picked at his food for several seconds before he finally began to eat with gusto.

"Aren't you eating?" he asked, noticing that all she had was coffee. "Junior needs his strength, too."

"Junior has prenatal vitamins," she said nonchalantly, tucking a strand of hair back into the French twist over her nape. "One of those, and I could lift the front end of a Mack truck."

He laughed faintly. His quiet eyes studied her as he finished off the steak and washed it down with black coffee.

"Did Dick send you over here?" he asked with a cynical smile.

"I came on my own," she replied.

"To save me from myself?" His voice was a little weak, but full of authority. He handed her the tray. "Thanks, but I can take care of myself."

"Of course you can, dear man," she agreed wholeheartedly, putting the tray on a side table. "Just look how well you were managing. How long had it been since you'd eaten?"

"I had a box of cheese crackers just yesterday," he assured her.

"Have you seen a doctor?" she persisted.

"What in God's name for?" he burst out. "I'm just tired!"

"You look feverish to me," she muttered. "And white as death."

"I had to finish the screenplay," he said wearily. His eyes held hers. "You should read it. It's the best thing I've ever done."

"I'll wait for the screen version, thanks," she said. "Can I get you anything else before I finish tidying up the living room?"

"You leave the living room alone," he said tersely. "I have a cleaning woman."

"If you did, she's dead of heart failure by now," she told him, rising. "It looks as if you've entertained a battalion of commandos in there."

"I was working!"

"No wonder you've never married," she muttered, lifting the tray from the table. "There isn't a woman anywhere brave enough to cope with this kind of mess."

"No? Then why are you here?" he asked gently.

She glanced at him with a calm expression. "When I figure it out, I'll let you know. Just one thing, Cul. I'm not dying of unrequited love anymore. You were right the whole time. We had a good physical relationship, but that's all it was. I realize that now."

He sat up straighter. "What are you talking about?"

"I've been doing some thinking," she said. "And I thought you'd like to know that I'm through mooning over you and accusing you of being my child's father." She even smiled at him. "Aren't you relieved?"

"I've done some thinking of my own," he began, choosing his words carefully. "Bett, about the baby..."

"All water under the bridge, darling," she broke in gaily. "Subject closed. Permanently." She started out the door with the tray.

"But, Bett...!"

"No," she returned, her voice firm. "Try to get some sleep, Cul. I'll finish up the dishes, and let myself out. All you needed was a decent meal and a little light housekeeping. You'll be fine now, I think."

"Why did you come?" he persisted, his green eyes quiet and intent.

She shrugged. "It's a great play. I'm working myself out of debt and having a blast in the process. I
figured I owed you one. So now we're even. Ciao."

She closed the door on his puzzled, exasperated
expression. She'd surprised herself with her new air of
maturity, her ability to cope without falling apart.
Amazing, that it had taken a broken heart and pregnancy to turn her life around. Now all she had to do
was pull herself together enough to go on without Cul.

How surprising that he'd been there all alone. He
had enough women that surely one or two of them
must have been willing to come and take care of him
while he was in seclusion. Maybe they only liked him
when he was a healthy man about town.

Cul was at the theater the next night, and he came
backstage after the performance to take her home.

"I usually do that," Janet said haughtily, glaring at
him as she waited for Bett to remove her makeup.

"From now on, I'll do it." He returned her look
steadily. "Any argument?"

"Now, see here, Cul..." Bett began hotly.

"No, no," he scolded. "Fighting is bad for the
baby. Hurry up. You need your rest."

"I'll see you tomorrow, then," Janet told Bett reluctantly. "Yell if you need me," she added with a
meaningful glance before she shot a last glare at Cul
and left.

"Bully," Bett accused him as she took off the last
of the makeup.

"It gets results," he said nonchalantly. He looked
well. Much more rested, less drawn, in well-fitting gray
slacks with a white shirt and red tie and a tweed jacket.
He was frankly sexy, and Bett didn't like remember-

ing the way those straining muscles felt under her exploring hands. He was extremely sensuous. He exicted her as no other man ever had. Especially now, when she carried his child in her body.

"Should you be out on the streets so soon?" she asked.

"I was only tired," he told her. "I feel much better, after your bit of nursing care."

"I can get home all by myself," she tried again, facing him in the brown jumper she wore for the performance.

"But you won't. Come on, little mama, I'll let you snuggle up to me if you get cold."

"In a Porsche, there's hardly enough room to do anything else," she muttered.

"Ahh, but I'm not driving the Porsche. I traded it this morning. For a Lincoln. More comfortable."

"I'd have thought the Porsche was exactly the thing for a happy bachelor," she remarked.

He opened the dressing room door for her. "I'm getting older, Bett. Too old to play around."

"Don't tell me you're thinking of settling down." She laughed. "I'd never believe it."

"Wouldn't you?"

She ignored that odd note in his tone and pulled her tweed coat closer around her as they went out into the cold night air.

"Is that the only coat you've got?" he asked curtly.

"It's warm," she replied.

"You need something with a hood."

"Great. Next year I'll ask Santa for one."

He sighed roughly as he led her to the big gray Lincoln parked outside the theater. "Why won't you let me do things for you?'' he asked quietly. "I'm sinfully rich. I have no one to spend the money on. I could get you anything you needed for the baby."

She glanced at him as he put her into the passenger seat of the car. "You wouldn't let me take care of you if the situation were reversed."

"That's different," he protested.

"Not different at all," she returned when he got in under the steering wheel. "You're as independent as I am, in your way."

"I thought you'd already admitted that the baby came first."

She leaned back in the seat. "Thanks to the company and the backers, I no longer have to worry myself sick about medical and grocery bills, thanks."

"There must be other things you want."

She smiled dreamily, closing her eyes as he drove, the sound of car engines and horns surrounding her. "Of course there are. I'd like those pretty pieces of baby furniture in the catalogs, and little frilly dresses for her to wear, and little patent leather shoes..."

"Her?" he asked softly, searching her face as he stopped at a traffic light.

"They did an amniocentesis test, along with ultrasound, to make sure there were no problems," she told him. "They can determine sex that way. She's a little girl, Cul."

He bit his lower lip hard enough to bruise it, his darkening green eyes dropping to the swell of her abdomen. He'd hit it right on the head that afternoon in the fast food grocery, musing about his daughter. And now it was his daughter, and he knew it, but Bett didn't want him anymore.

"Thought about names?" he asked with apparent carelessness as he pulled back into traffic.

"I like Kathryn. Kate for short."

He considered that with a smile. "How about Elisabet?" he asked dryly.

"One is enough," she muttered. "Anyway, I've always liked Helen. It's my mother's name."

"Add an 'e' on the end and it sounds better. Kathryn Helene."

"Yes. I like that." She studied her hands in her lap. "What was your mother's name?"

"Michele," he said tersely.

"And your father's?"

"Thomas."

There was a coldness in his tone that puzzled her. "Are they still alive?"

"He died somewhere in France, where he was 'entertaining' two teenage girls. My mother wound up in a retreat for alcoholics. I visit her once or twice a year."

"I'm sorry. It must have been a pretty rough life."

"Boarding schools, mostly," he replied. "They never wanted children. I was an accident, and they told me so, frequently. I was an unwanted infringement on their leisure time, so I was promptly dispatched to boarding school at the age of six. It was the best thing, considering the circumstances. I never even missed them."

But he had, Bett thought, studying him. He'd missed having someone to love him and care about him.

"Are you feeling all right?" he asked unexpectedly. "This production isn't putting you at risk?"

She smiled. "It's actually doing me a lot of good. I get my daily exercise, I have no time to sit around and brood about what might go wrong, and I'm doing exactly what my doctor says to do the rest of the time. I'm fine."

"I'll make sure of that, from now on," he said with dogged determination. "I'm going to be your shadow."

"I'm fine," she insisted. "Listen, Cul, I'm perfectly capable of looking out for myself and the baby. I'm not your responsibility."

"You are," he returned.

"I'm not asking for anything. I told you last night, I don't feel that way about you anymore, Cul."

His expression was shocked, but he averted his face so that she couldn't see it. "You'll never forget what I said to you when you told me, will you?" he asked quietly.

"It was pretty rough," she confessed. Her eyes had a faraway look in their dark depths as she folded her hands in her lap and stared out at the city lights. "I was so excited," she recalled, her smile wistful. "It seemed like the end of the rainbow. And then you wouldn't even listen to me. I think that hurt most of all. Now, of course, I can understand why you didn't believe me. But it doesn't matter anymore."

"You're sure that Hadison doesn't want to marry you?" he asked hesitantly.

"I'm sure." She grinned. "I think he'll eventually marry Janet, actually. They'll make a good couple, too."

"Then what about the baby?"

"I'll take good care of her. Why should I share her?"

"She needs a father," he argued curtly. "Someone to screen her boyfriends when she's older and comfort her when she cries in the night."

"I can do all that," Bett assured him.

"Not like a father could!"

She pretended to think about that. "I'll let Mr. Bartholomew screen them."

"He'll be dead by then!"

"Don't shout, Cul, what will my neighbors think?" she protested. They were parked just below her apartment window, and Cul's face was red with bottled-up fury.

"You could marry me," he said. "We could both raise her."

"No, thank you," she replied politely.

"She's my child!" he burst out.

She looked him straight in the eye. "No," she said coldly. "You won't get around me that way, by pretending to believe me at this late date. You won't convince me that you've had such a sudden change of heart."

"But I have," he began.

"I'm very tired, Cul," she said wearily, "and I don't feel up to any arguments tonight. Thanks for bringing me home."

He got out of the car and went around to open her door, his face taut with indecision, his eyes dark with mingled hunger and frustration.

She took the hand he extended, feeling a pleasant tingle at its warm strength as he helped her out onto the sidewalk. He didn't let it go, either, retaining it even after he locked the door and walked her up to her apartment.

"I'd feel better about it if you'd move in with me," he said as he left her at her door. "Even if you won't marry me, you'd be safe."

"Protected, no doubt, by your legion of lady lovers?"

"I don't have any lovers, Bett," he replied, his voice deep and soft.

"And the pope isn't Catholic," she agreed.

"Now who's lacking trust?" he queried.

"I've been getting lessons." She unlocked her door and stared down at the rusty doorknob. "Thanks again for seeing me home."

He touched her shoulder lightly. He turned her around, pulled her gently against his tall, strong body and looked down into her wide, dark eyes.

"I'm going to take care of you, Bett. Even if you fight me every step of the way."

"Cul..."

"Shhhh," he whispered gently, bending so that she could taste the minty scent of his breath on her parted lips. "Sleep tight, darling."

He made the endearment sound genuine. And she didn't protest when he laid his warm, firm mouth over hers and gently nibbled at it. It was so sweet, that tenderness from him, that giving. Always before, even when he was the most gentle, he was still taking, not giving. This was different.

He lifted his head a breath later and touched his fingers to her cheek. "Good night, Elisabet."

"Good night."

She watched him walk away with tears in her eyes. Oh, Cul, she thought miserably, why are you pretending to believe me now, when you were so determined not to believe me in the beginning? How can I ever trust you again?

He seemed to sense her eyes on his back, because he suddenly turned and looked at her across the distance. And he smiled, slowly, and lifted his hand before he turned the corner. She turned slowly and went into the apartment, her mind full of questions.

Ten

You don't really believe he's had a change of heart, do you?" Janet asked Bett the next morning as they had coffee together in the little deli down the street from Bett's apartment.

"No," Bett confessed. "I think he just wants the baby. You know how wild he's always been about children. Since no other man has jumped in to claim it, he's going to."

Janet stared into her black coffee. "Don't let him cut you up a second time," she said gently.

"Don't worry, he won't get close enough for that." Bett stirred cream into her own coffee. "You know, it's odd, but I learned more about him last night than I've ever known. He actually talked to me. And it made me realize that he never had before. Even when we were so involved with each other.''

''Well, with any luck at all, he'll at least live up to his responsibilities. Imagine him thinking it was David's baby!''

Bett lifted her eyes and studied her friend. ''It isn't, you know,'' she said levelly. ''David is my friend. He's never been anything else, so you can stop worrying yourself to death about it.''

Janet blushed wildly. ''Oh, Bett, I didn't mean...!''

Bett actually laughed. ''You silly twit,'' she accused. ''You know I've been crazy about Cul for years. Not even for revenge could I sleep with someone else.''

''I knew that, deep down. I guess I just wanted to hear you say it,'' Janet confessed.

''So now I have. Okay?'' She shook her head and leaned back in her chair. ''Oh, Janet, what am I going to do with...oof!'' She put a hand to her stomach and caught her breath, looking dazed.

''What's wrong?'' Janet asked quickly.

''The baby kicked,'' she said breathlessly, laughing with tears in her eyes. ''Oh, my!''

''For heaven's sake!'' Janet was mystified.

''They move around, you know. You really start to feel them about four and a half months.'' She sighed as she smoothed her hand over the soft mound. ''Imagine. I'm really going to be a mother. Of all the incredible things...''

''Speaking of incredible things, don't look now, but here comes trouble.''

Bett turned to see Cul searching the deli for her. He found her and moved quickly toward them, a tall, formidable figure in a blue pinstriped suit.

"What are you doing here?" he asked, taking a seat beside Bett.

"Having breakfast. I always have breakfast here," she bristled.

"You like bagels and cream cheese for breakfast?" he asked. "Okay. Marry me, and I'll buy you the place."

Bett flushed and Janet's eyes widened.

Cul directed his next speech to Janet. "I've asked her ten times," he said. "I've proposed at breakfast, lunch and dinner. I've proposed drunk and sober. She won't marry me. Will you please tell her that I'm rich? I can give her anything she wants. I can give the baby a good education and dress her like a little princess. I can even," he added slyly, "take care of the baby's mama. If she'd just marry me!"

Two rough-looking men at the next table overheard him and turned around. Anything was better than the usual dull routine of coffee and bagels.

"Hey, lady, you got a screw loose?" one of them asked. "He ain't bad looking. And babies need lots of stuff."

"That's right," the shorter, darker man agreed. "My wife and I raised six. Let me tell you, diapers don't come cheap!"

"Worst of all, it's my baby," Cul told the men on a soft sigh. "She won't marry me and give it a name. It's a little girl."

"Awwww," the bigger man murmured, smiling. "That's sweet."

"Yeah." The shorter one grinned. "I got two little girls of my own."

"You oughta marry him, honey," the bigger man told Bett. "All this talk about people living together and all—it ain't right. Parents ought to be married. Kids notice stuff like that, you know. They make it rough on each other."

"He doesn't believe it's his baby," Bett told them.

"I do so," Cul shot back.

"No you don't," Bett said shortly. "You're just saying that, to make me marry you. You feel sorry for me!"

"Will you just for once listen to me?" Cul demanded.

"Here, now, don't go upsetting the girl," the man at the next table threatened. "She's delicate."

"That's right, I'm delicate," Bett told Cul with a curt nod of her head.

"You'll be more delicate if you don't start eating a decent breakfast," Cul returned. "You need bacon and eggs and toast and such."

"Well, he's got a point there," the short man at the next table agreed. "Babies need a lot of nourishment."

"I'll say," the waitress agreed, pausing to refill coffee cups. "I'll never forget how hungry I used to get when I carried mine."

"My old lady says the same thing," the bigger man agreed, pulling his hat further over his bald head and moving his chair closer. "You get heartburn yet, honey?"

"Yes . . ." Bett began.

"Nothing like a bottle of Maalox to fix that," the big man told her.

The shorter one moved his chair closer, too, forcing Cul to move right up against Bett. He grinned and put an arm around her as the waitress drew up a chair and sat down, and they discussed everything from heartburn to politics to theater.

"I thought you looked familiar," the big man nodded when he discovered who Bett was. "Everybody's been talking about that play. And your feller wrote it, huh? Must be smart."

"Not so smart," Cul sighed, dropping a careless kiss on Bett's hair, "or I could get her to marry me."

"What kind of life would she have," Janet muttered at him, "with your long line of girlfriends in the background?"

"I don't have a long line of girlfriends," Cul told her. "I've reformed. I'm going to be a model husband and father."

"I've already told you, I'm not marrying you," Bett told him firmly.

"We'll see about that," Cul returned.

"No, we won't . . . oooof!" She jerked back again as the baby kicked and knocked the wind out of her.

"What happened?" Cul asked, wide-eyed.

"The baby kicked," Janet said knowledgeably. "They do kick, you know."

"Awwww," the big man next to Cul said again, smiling. "Ain't that sweet? My oldest boy used to kick up a storm in my wife's stomach."

Cul hardly heard the others launch into a discussion of kicking babies. He was staring at Bett, and the two of them were in a world of their own.

She took his big hand and carried it to her abdomen, pressing it firmly against the mound, slightly to the side of her diaphragm. She bit her lip, waiting, and the baby kicked again. And he felt it.

His face seemed to glow. His eyes softened as they met hers. He smiled, so tenderly. "My God," he whispered.

She smiled back. "She's very strong, isn't she?" she asked gently. "The doctor says it's a good sign that she's active so soon."

Cul searched her eyes. "Magic," he said under his breath. "That two people can create something so beautiful."

Yes, she thought, if only he believed that it was truly his child and not someone else's. She couldn't believe that he'd changed his mind so radically, because nothing had changed. She was certain that he still had doubts.

Around them, the others were still on the subject of pregnancy. They hardly noticed when Cul drew Bett up with him, nodded to Janet, and led her out onto the street.

"Where are we going?" Bett asked him.

He had her hand tight in his and he curled his fingers into hers, smiling down at her. "I thought we might go look through the baby department at Macy's."

She tingled all over. "But..."

"Listen—" he said, turning her to face him so that they blocked traffic, a big blond man with a red-headed pregnant woman in his grasp "—a baby is a baby. You've got one and I want one. So if you'll let me help you raise her, I'll spoil her rotten."

Her lips parted and he bent and kissed her with exquisite tenderness, sending swirls of pleasure all through her.

"But . . ." she tried again.

"You want me, Bett," he said softly, searching her dark eyes with his green ones. "And I want you, and this." He touched her abdomen gently. "We've got so much going for us, darling. A mutual love of theater, a love of children, an attraction that never seems to fade, and mutual respect. Isn't that enough to start with?"

She bit her lower lip. The baby did need a name. And she needed Cul. But how could she marry him when he thought she was carrying another man's child? She looked up, worried, with the fear in her eyes.

"I care about you," he said soberly. "I want to look after you and the baby."

She stared at his tie. It was nice. Burgundy with little round things on it. "You don't want to get married."

"Oh, but I do," he breathed fervently. He cupped her face in his hands and lifted it to blazing green eyes. "I do, I do . . . you don't know how much!"

He bent and pressed her soft lips apart with his, probing, gently nibbling. She felt her knees going weak and caught his big arms to keep from going down. He smiled against her warm mouth.

"Getting weak in the knees, little one?" he whispered on a rough laugh. "Come home with me, and I'll love you half to death, Bett."

That did make her blood sing. She caught her breath. "You can't go around propositioning pregnant women in the middle of the street."

"I just did. Come on," he taunted, biting gently at her lower lip, tugging it between his teeth. "I'll nibble your breasts like this, Bett, just the way you like it."

She trembled. "Cul!"

His cheek nuzzled hers and his breath was warm at her ear. "Come home with me, you little coward. You know you want to."

"I have a matinee..." she began.

"Your understudy is going on for you," he murmured. "I want you all to myself for a while. Just the two of us. The three of us," he amended, tracing her belly with his fingers. "Well?"

Her nails bit into the fine fabric of his suit coat. Her eyes closed. Where were her pride and her temper when she needed them?

"Yes," she said on a held breath. He turned her, clasping her hand tightly, and drew her along with him.

Minutes later, she found herself in his apartment without any real sense of how she got there. He had her across his lap on the sofa, and he was kissing her like a starving man.

"Did you know," he murmured between kisses, "that possession is nine-tenths of the law?

"What do you mean?"

"That I've got you now, and I'm not letting you out of this apartment," he chuckled under his breath. "You're mine."

"Kidnapper!" she accused.

"When it's the only recourse left," he agreed. His hands eased her out of the tweed coat, disclosing the burgundy corduroy maternity skirt and the patterned maternity top that matched it.

She touched his hand as he started to remove the top. "Cul, I'm awfully swollen," she said apprehensively.

"And you don't think I'll find you sexy like this?" he mused, studying her wide eyes. "Idiot!"

He picked her up, laughing, carrying her into his bedroom. He eased her down onto the coverlet, and stripped her with deft, expert hands, disclosing a body that was exquisite in pregnancy, all cream and mauve contrasts and rounded flesh.

"Don't you know," he whispered, touching her stomach, her breasts, "that there's nothing more beautiful than a rose in full bloom?"

She bit her lower lip. "I'll get bigger."

"Hallelujah!" he said on a beaming smile. "More of you to hold."

Tears misted her eyes. "You don't think I look ugly?"

"Wait until I get my clothes off, honey, and I'll show you what I think."

He undressed slowly, letting her watch, laughing deeply at her fascination. This was new, because even during their earlier intimacy, he'd never undressed for her. There had always been too much urgency.

But now he was taking his time, taunting her with the threat of his big, hard-muscled body.

"Want me, Bett?" he chided as the last vestiges of clothing came away and he stood over her, hands on his hips, challenging her.

Her eyes adored him. Her lover. The father of her child. Her whole world. "More than I want to go on breathing," she whispered, absently.

He sat down beside her and drew her hands to his chest, brushing them over the thick hair and warm muscle, watching them learn the contours of his body. "We never did it like this, did we, Bett?" he whispered as he taught her how to touch him, to please him. "We never did it with love."

She caught her breath. "I did."

"Yes. But I didn't," he whispered, bending to her mouth. "Not like this."

And when he began to kiss her, she knew the difference immediately. It was a kind of wooing. A tender wooing. A tasting of souls more than bodies, mutual consideration and selflessness. Her heart seemed to stop beating altogether at the new and gentle passion he gave her.

She felt the rough-silk slide of his body on hers, the aching tenderness of his mouth learning every curve, every line of her body. He was slower than he'd ever been, more thorough. And in every soft brush of his lips was the emotion that had been lacking before. The love.

"Exquisite," he whispered huskily as his mouth edged down her waist to her hips and over the mound of their child. "I never knew anything could be as profound as this!"

He was trembling all over, and still he continued, touching her writhing body as if he'd never touched a woman in his life. She moaned helplessly, giving herself to him, trusting her pleasure to the expert hands and mouth that were schooling her body in delicious agony.

"Cul, please!" Her voice broke. Her eyes, looking up into his, were wild and darker than onyx, her body as taut as steel under the guiding touch of his hands.

His own eyes were glittering strangely, his face drawn, reddened with contained passion. He smiled slowly as he lifted up and drew her hips gently under his.

"Is it unbearable, Bett?" he whispered. "Is that why you're trembling so madly under me?"

"Un . . . bearable," she agreed, gasping. Her hands went to his hips and tried to pull them down to the ache in her own. "I want . . . you . . . so, Cul!"

He looked down at her body, sliding his big hands under her, lifting her. "No," he whispered when she tried to rush him. "No, lie still. Let me do it. Let me control it. Look, darling. Watch us."

She did, her eyes widening in astonishment, because it had never been quite so intimate before. "Cul!"

"Good," he breathed, his eyes closing, his mouth opening. "Good. It's good. It's so good this time, so good! Bett!"

She barely heard him. Her body was on fire, quicksilver under the sweet crush of his, feeling his heartbeat over hers, his fierce movements echoing the taut writhing of her own.

He was groaning, and she twisted up toward him, reaching for a fulfillment that would surely kill her. And it was happening. All at once, in a sunburst of explosive passion, it was happening. She began to weep as it washed over her, taking her mind, flinging her up against his damp, shuddering body. She heard him cry out hoarsely seconds later, and their frantic heartbeats seemed amplified, filling the room, deafening her....

She felt his mouth on her closed eyelids, her forehead, her cheeks, her throat. He was kissing her, comforting her, drying the tears.

Her eyes opened, astonished, and looked up into a face so warm and tender with love that she started crying all over again.

He laughed, the sound soft and sweet, and he drew a corner of the sheet against her cheeks to absorb the salty tears. "I hope my neighbors are away," he whispered with wicked humor, "or the police may be at our doorstep any minute to find out who's being tortured in here."

"I couldn't help it," she muttered, coloring.

"Neither could I," he whispered, bending to kiss her swollen mouth tenderly. "Oh, darling, such sweet explosions! We never loved like that."

She held him to her, staring past his damp blond head at the ceiling. "No," she said quietly. "Not like that."

"I didn't even know that I loved you, Bett," he whispered at her ear, "until you accused me of not knowing how. Until you told me to go away, and I realized that I was going to die without you. And it was too late. Or so I thought."

Her heart leaped. She knew that he loved her, of
course. After what had just happened, it was impossible not to know. But it was so wonderful to hear it.

She held him closer, smoothing his cool, damp hair
with long, loving fingers. "Those were dark days,
without you," she whispered.

His hands contracted at her back. "And I left you
to face it all alone. Pregnancy and illness..." His voice
broke.

"It's all right," she whispered, cherishing him
against her. "It's all right. I understand."

"No, you don't." He drew away from her slowly,
with a deep breath, and reached for a cigarette. He
propped himself up, magnificent in his unashamed
nudity, and drew her to his side while he smoked.
"Bett, what you said about my reasoning...most of
it was true. I didn't realize it, but I was using my sterility as a weapon, to keep out of emotional involvement. My parents weren't the ideal endorsement for
marriage and commitment, you know. They had af-
fairs all my life. I never knew a loving family or security. I never had either. I thought I wanted it, but I
kept drawing back, out of fear." He looked down at
her. "I was afraid of loving you, because I was afraid
of losing you."

She let her head fall back on his arm and looked up
at him with a teasing grin. "If you'd only known. I'd
have followed you through a forest fire with matches
in both hands. That never changed, in all the years
between. Why do you think I was still a virgin?"

"I didn't let myself think about it. It was too re-
vealing, because I realized how much it mattered to
me, being your first man." He touched her soft belly,

and smiled broadly. "And now...our daughter. My God, you'll never know the names I called myself when I thought I'd lost you and the baby. I've been in hell since the afternoon I stormed out of your apartment. I was terrified that you might go off half cocked and marry someone, just for security."

"So you locked yourself up in your tower and got drunk?"

"Not quite," he confessed. "Actually, I was working on something."

He put out the cigarette and got up, disappearing into the other room. He was back a minute later with a manuscript in one hand. He tossed it onto the bed and stretched out on his stomach beside her.

"Read that," he murmured, "while I take a cat-nap. When I wake up," he added, opening one eye, "we'll make feverish love, followed by feverish marriage plans."

She opened her mouth to speak, but he chided, "Read, woman, read!"

And for the next hour, she did. It was a copy of his screenplay. It opened with a couple of struggling actors in a small summer stock theater group, and the hero was sterile. His lover became pregnant, and he wouldn't believe the baby was his. But in the end, without having fertility tests rerun or any other scientific proof offered, he realized that trust was the important thing. Either he loved her enough to take her word, or he didn't love her at all. He decided that the baby was his. And they married, after a turbulent courtship, and lived happily ever after with the twins she bore him.

She stared at the scattered pages for a long moment, before she realized that it was their story. Cul was telling her that he did believe it was his baby, despite proof to the contrary. He was telling her, for all the world to see, that he loved her.

Tears began to trickle down her cheeks. She felt humble.

"Now, now, little mama, don't cry," he whispered, rolling over to draw her down into his arms. "You'll upset little Kate."

She cried all the harder. "Oh, Cul," she whimpered against his warm, strong shoulder. "I love you so!"

"Do you really?" he murmured. "Why don't you roll over and show me, then? And then I'll show you, and afterward we'll call your parents and tell them that they're going to have a son-in-law and a grandbaby."

She sniffed into a corner of the sheet. "They'll be scandalized." she said, laughing tearfully.

"They'll be too delighted to be scandalized. Come on, weeping willow," he teased, easing her onto his bare chest, so that her breasts became sensitive to the exquisite abrasion of his hair. "Make love to me."

"But I don't know how," she protested shyly. "You never liked me to take the initiative."

"That was before I realized why I'd walked around like half a man ever since Atlanta," he murmured softly. His eyes caressed hers. "Oh, Bett, there was never another woman. There were a few casual pick-ups, but any man can tell you that lust alone is very unsatisfying. Eventually, I gave up sex for companionship. Until you came along again, that is. And now, I want to do everything with you. I want to live with you and love you and spoil you rotten. I want to plan things with you, and look forward to the baby with you." He brushed her mouth with his. "I want to grow old with you, darling woman."

"I want to grow old with you, too," she whispered.

"But not right away," he murmured, easing her body fully onto his. "We've got a lot of experimenting to do. Now, first you put this hand, here." He laughed at her shocked exclamation. "That's it. Now sit up, darling . . . my God, what an expression! Sweet angel, didn't you realize that we could change positions occasionally? Don't faint just yet, Bett, let me show you . . . yes! Oh, yes, darling, yes . . . !"

"But Cul . . . !" she groaned.

He put his hands on her hips and helped her, and all too soon she realized that he couldn't hear her. She gave in to the sensations that were clouding her mind and let him teach her.

Bett couldn't remember a time in her entire life that she'd been as happy as she was in the days that followed. She moved in with Cul and they were married by a justice of the peace, with Janet and David for witnesses.

She and Cul were inseparable. They shopped together for the baby, they went places together, he sat backstage and watched to make sure she didn't tire herself during the performances. And the baby grew and grew, like the love that linked her parents.

"I think she's going to be a baseball team when she grows up," Bett gasped one night several months later, holding her enormous belly after an especially grueling performance. "Did you see her kick?"

"I did, indeed," Cul chuckled, hugging her. "Any day now, didn't the doctor say?"

"Well, judging by what I was feeling during the last two acts, I think it could be any minute now," Bett gasped as another pain hit her.

Cul went pasty. Janet and David came walking up behind him, gaping at his expression.

"What's up?" David asked.

"She's having the baby," Cul said in a hushed, horrified tone. "Oh, my God, she's having the baby. What do I do?"

If the pain hadn't been so intense, Bett would have doubled over laughing. Imagine Cul, always so capable and masterful, standing there asking what to do!

"Hospital," Bett gasped, holding on to his arm. "Quick, darling!"

"I left the car at home," Cul burst out.

"Cab," Bett managed. The pain was blinding.

"We'll get one," Janet said, pulling David along. "Bring her to the side door, Cul, we'll get one if we have to hijack it!"

Cul picked her up, his arms strong and sure despite her weight, and carried her to the side door.

"It's all right, darling, it's all right," he kept repeating as he hurried along. "I'll get you to the hospital, it's all right."

David and Janet had kidnapped a cab, by the look of them, one standing in front of it, the other holding the back door open.

"My God, it's you!" the big, burly cabdriver grinned, recognizing his companions from the deli. "Is it time?"

"It's time," Cul groaned. "Oh, for God's sake, hurry!"

David and Janet piled into the cab, too.

"Which hospital?" the cabbie asked.

"I—I forget! Something General—" Cul agonized, green eyes staring horrified into the cabbie's. "Which hospital?" he asked Janet and David.

"We don't know, either!" Janet burst out, staring at Bett's contorted face.

"Take us to any hospital!" Cul demanded.

"City...General," Bett told the cabdriver.

"All right, little lady!" He grinned, pulling out into traffic. "Hold on, now." And he stood on the accelerator.

"What if we don't make it in time?" Cul asked. "What will we do?"

"Deliver it ourselves," the cabbie said.

"Heavens, no!" Janet exclaimed, both hands at her cheeks. "I couldn't!

"Me, neither," David groaned.

Cul swallowed. "Well, don't look at me, I'm a playwright!"

"Let's all sing," the cabbie suggested. "Come on, it will help her. Here we go. Row, row, row your boat...!" He sang gaily, gesturing for the others to join in. "Come on, it will relax you!"

So they sang, loudly, as the cabbie took the curb on two wheels, almost right into the back of a police car. Sirens flared, lights flashed.

"No!" Cul groaned.

The cabbie stopped quickly and rolled down the window. "Help!" he yelled as the policeman came back to lean in the window. "This is the very pregnant actress who was in *Girl in a Dark Room* that's on Broadway, there's the guy that wrote it, and the other guy is the male lead. We got a baby girl who wants to be born, and if I don't make it to City General in about two minutes..."

"You just follow me!" The policeman grinned. "Hang on, honey," he told Bett. "I've seen the play twice already. You were great!"

She tried to thank him, but he was climbing into his squad car and revving up.

"All together now," the cabbie called over his shoulder as he screeched off in mad pursuit. "Row, row, row your boat...!"

And they rowed and rowed until the hospital emergency room came careering into view.

Eleven

Less than an hour after they got to the hospital, little Kate was born, weighing in at just over eight pounds. Thanks to the natural childbirth classes that Cul and Bett had taken, it wasn't too difficult a delivery. And the best thing was that Cul had been with her every step of the way. He hadn't left her until the baby was placed just briefly in his gloved hands and he looked at her with tears in his eyes. Through waves of pain, Bett smiled up at the two of them. My world, she thought.

Cul went out into the waiting room minutes later to find the cabdriver, the policeman, Janet and David, the other man from the Deli, and its waitress, and Mr. Bartholomew and half the cast of *Girl in a Dark Room* waiting for news.

He burst out laughing as he watched them avidly discussing the play together, and thought, only in New York....

"Well?" Dick Hamilton burst out, rising. "What is it?"

The others turned their attention to Cul. "What is it?" they echoed.

"The best production of my life," he said with a grin. "Kathryn Helene McCullough. She weighs eight pounds, and she's twenty inches long, and she has all her fingers and toes!"

Congratulations went the rounds. The cabdriver produced a box of pink-wrapped cigars from somewhere and presented them to Cul, who dispensed them all around.

"Coffee's on me!" Cul announced and led the way to the hot drinks machine. Well, he reasoned, the policeman couldn't drink on duty, after all, and where would he get a bottle of champagne in a hospital? So little Kate was toasted with black coffee and hot chocolate.

Later, sitting in a chair by Bett's bed, Cul watched the tiny infant suckle at her mother's breast with tears in his eyes.

"So beautiful," he whispered, brushing his fingers lightly over the tiny head with its scattering of blond hair. "So beautiful."

Bett looked up at him and smiled wearily. "Isn't she precious?" she whispered. "Imagine. We did that."

He nodded, sighing contentedly. "The waiting room was full," he told her. "I passed out cigars."

"Wherever did you get them?" she asked.

"The cabdriver. Mr. Bartholomew came, too, and I phoned your parents. They're flying up."

"Is mother well enough?" she asked, concerned.

"Your mother has been taking her medicine, for a change," Cul replied, "and your father says she's better than ever. He expects that he's going to die of exhaustion any day now from keeping up with her renewed ardor." Bett actually blushed. It was hard to think about her parents doing that sort of thing.

"Well, they were like us once," he reminded her. "Young, holding their firstborn in their arms." He studied the baby at her breast. "I'm glad you decided to do that," he added. "Somehow, a bottle isn't quite the same."

"The doctor says that babies get a lot of immunity from nursing," she said. "I thought that might give little Kate a head start."

"And besides all that," he said with a tender light in his eyes, "it's exquisite to watch."

She smiled, not offended. "Did you thank the cabdriver and the policeman for getting us here in time?"

"I'm buying them both breakfast. Along with David and Janet. At the deli tomorrow morning," he grinned. "You'll get your breakfast here and so will baby."

"You're a nice man, Mr. McCullough. I'm glad I married you."

He bent and kissed her dry lips softly. "That works both ways. She's beautiful. Like her mama."

She searched his eyes quietly, and wondered if he'd truly accepted that she was his daughter...wondered if he had any lingering doubts.

He smoothed away the frown between her eyes. "I was wondering," he murmured.

"Wondering what?" she asked softly.

He glanced down at the baby against her creamy skin. "Well, they said once would be impossible, and it wasn't. So I wondered... Do you suppose we might try again and see if we could make a boy next time, so that we'd have a matched set?" he asked with a faint grin.

Her eyes misted again. "Oh, Cul, I love you."

He bent to her warm mouth. "I love you, too." He tasted tears on her mouth when he kissed her, and smiled against her warm lips. Now, finally, she believed him.

He wasn't totally convinced. It was hard to accept, that a specialist could be wrong about his sterility. On the other hand, he couldn't imagine Bett sleeping with any other man. She had a basic honesty that would have insisted she tell him, if that had been the case. But she was certain the baby was Cul's and he accepted it at face value. Once, he even considered having the fertility test done again, but that would prove he didn't believe Bett. It would raise more barriers, and he didn't want that. So he simply accepted. And settled into family life with a flair.

Over a year passed, and Cul's screenplay had just gone into full production. He was away for a couple of months on and off, seeing that things were going all right. And Bett was still starring on Broadway in *Girl in a Dark Room*. Janet and David were engaged and soon to be married, and baby Kate had her own private nanny who kept her backstage while mama played to a packed audience.

It was spring, and everything was bursting into blossom, and Bett waited for Cul to come home with a new and mysterious radiance.

"You look more beautiful every day," Cul said when she ran to meet him at the airport. His green eyes wandered over her possessively, lovingly. "Miss me?"

"Terriby." She reached up and kissed him warmly, doing sensuous things to his mouth with hers until she felt the telltale tremble in his tall, strong body. "Baby Kate is visiting grandma and grandpa in their hotel room at the Roosevelt. Nanny is off for the day. Our housekeeper finished at noon and went home. And I," she breathed into his mouth, "have this overpowering urge to make passionate love on the living room carpet with all the windows open."

"Bett, for God's sake," he groaned laughingly, his body making emphatic statements about his own needs.

"You do seem to be interested." She grinned. "Come home with me, darling," she vamped.

"I hope we have time to get there," he said uncomfortably, clearing his throat as he steered her quickly out of the terminal.

It had been several weeks since they'd had any length of time alone, and they reacted to it with a sweeping passion. She couldn't remember a time when they'd been so desperate for each other. Her teasing remark about the living-room carpet became reality the minute they got into the apartment, because they couldn't make it any farther.

He lowered her to the floor and crushed her into the carpeting with the hard weight of his body, his mouth devouring hers in the stillness as he kissed her.

"I can't wait," he whispered huskily. "I'm sorry, darling, I'll make it up to you, but I can't . . . hold it."

"Take me," she whispered back, her eyes feverish, her hands holding him, helping him as he got only the necessary things out of his way before he pushed roughly down against her.

He caught his breath at the ease of his path, at the quick, hard rhythm that her body quickly caught up and followed. Jungle drums, she thought, looking into the forest of his eyes. Jungle drums, throbbing, throbbing. . . .

Her voice broke as he caught her hips with his hands and jerked them upward, his body hard and heavy as it surged downward, his groan throbbing like his body, like her own as they moved fiercely together and felt the fever burst over them both at once.

She was aware of the dampness of his body, the softness of his voice at her ear, asking if she was all right, if he'd hurt her.

"Hurt me?" she laughed softly. "Oh, darling!"

He lifted his head, trembling, and looked down into her dark, soft eyes, and then at her body, which was still half clothed. "Well, my God, talk about minute men . . ." He laughed at his own urgency.

"Desperation," she grinned wickedly. "Now carry me to bed and let's do it properly. If you're still able?" she teased.

"I'll show you who's able," he replied with pure male malice, and carried her into the bedroom.''

He tossed her on the bed and proved his stamina in ways that left her gasping and trembling all over before he finally gave her the fulfillment she eventually begged him for.

"You were making some insulting remark about my stamina, I believe?" he murmured an hour later, leaning over her propped on an elbow, covered with sweat.

She could just barely breathe. "I'm dead," she told him. "I know I am. No one could have lived through that."

He chuckled, brushing her mouth with his. "This is what comes of spending two weeks away from you. I was half dead with hunger."

"Good," she laughed. "Now I know you weren't indulging yourself with those little starlets."

"As if one of them could ever satisfy me." He chuckled at the old joke between them. "Feeling all right?"

"If you only knew," she sighed. She lay back, full of dreams. She had something to tell him that was so sweet, she just closed her eyes and savored it for several long moments.

"You're very quiet," he murmured, tracing her mouth with his finger.

She opened her eyes and looked up into his, with all her heart showing. "Darling," she began slowly, touching the damp mat of hair over his hard chest, "do you remember asking me once if we could make a boy?"

He sighed gently. "Yes. But, sweet, we can always adopt one," he told her, and there was no bitterness in his tone now, no anger. He smiled. "One miracle in a lifetime is enough, and you know how I adore our Kate. I wouldn't trade her for a boy."

"That isn't quite what I meant." She tugged at a curling wisp of dark blond hair. "I went to see my doctor today."

He didn't move. He didn't breathe. His taut body lay frozen beside her as he waited. "And?"

Her eyes warmed, bursting with color and light and feeling. "Oh, Cul, can't you guess?" she whispered. "Can't you? I'm pregnant!"

He opened his mouth to speak, and had to swallow first. He jerked her close in his arms to hold her bruisingly against his warm bareness, his head bent over hers, his entire body trembling with mingled delight and love. Because now there were no doubts left, not one. Their marriage had been heaven on earth, so close to one another that a night's separation was torment.

Tears were burning her own eyes and she nuzzled her damp face into his warm throat. "It must be the water," she laughed brokenly, clinging. "Either that, or we have an angel sitting on our shoulders. Cul, we really must send your doctor a birth announcement this time!"

"Yes, I should think so," he whispered huskily. "Darling, I love you! Adore you!"

"I love you, too," she breathed at his ear. "And if you ever needed proof, you have it now."

His mouth searched for hers and kissed it warmly, tasting tears. "Didn't you think Kate's green eyes were proof enough?" he murmured delightedly. He lifted his head, and his eyes cherished her. "I love you. That, for me, means trust. The day I realized what you meant to me was the end of all my doubts."

She touched his hard face with loving hands, smiling up at him. "Sometimes I thought you would never admit it," she confessed. "There always seemed to be something missing, those first days we were lovers."

"But I loved you even then," he said. "I'd gotten so accustomed to being alone that I wasn't sure I could let another person into my life. Especially a woman. But you'll never know how it was in California."

She pinched him. "Yes, with that Cherrie person..."

He nibbled her lower lip. "I never told you, did I, that Cherrie and her husband owned the beach house where I was staying? Bob and I went to school together."

Her mouth fell open. "What?"

He pushed her back down again, grinning. "Men have to have a few secrets." He smoothed her tumbled red-gold hair away from her face. "Did you know you have freckles right there?" He kissed the bridge of her nose.

"Stop that. How can I argue with you when you're kissing me?" she muttered.

"I don't want to argue."

"But you let me think you were having a red-hot affair!" she persisted.

He lifted her palm to his warm mouth. "I was trying to run you off. You had such a hold on me, Bett. Those long, exquisite nights in my bed had left me grieving for you. I loved you, so desperately. I didn't rush back for opening night to see how my play was going to fare, I rushed back to see you."

"With that gorgeous Tammy on your arm," she recalled.

"Window dressing. My shield, to keep you from seeing how hooked I really was. In fact, I was hooked in Atlanta. I just convinced myself that it was only physical."

"You had me convinced, too, after opening night," she said dryly.

He shook his head slowly, watching her. "I thought I was going to die when you told me you were pregnant. I was sure it wasn't mine. But I was equally sure you hadn't cheated on me. It made for some interesting mental exercises in logic. Finally, I decided that if I loved you, truly loved you, trust was the proof of it. And just when I was ready to tell you that, you stopped caring. At least, you stopped listening. I went off to write my screenplay, to show you I meant it, certain that you hated me by then. And all of a sudden, there you were on my doorstep, saving me from certain dissolution." He smiled. "Then I knew there was a little hope left, so I started chasing you. And got explosive results."

She remembered that feverish lovemaking, the sweetness of finally knowing she was loved. Reading the screenplay, realizing what she meant to him...her eyes went soft with memory.

"The only regret I have," he continued, "is that I didn't marry you in the very beginning. Your parents are still a little unhappy about the sequence of things, and I can't say I blame them. Kate won't be allowed to sleep with men until she's married," he added doggedly. "And society be damned."

"Why, just listen to you!" she chided. "Just listen! How pious you've become!"

"It's your fault. Who's been dragging me to church every Sunday. Which reminds me," he glared at her, "does Bartholomew have to come with us?"

"He's getting older," she reminded him. "It's hard for him to find the cab fare. Besides, you know he adores his goddaughter." She traced a pattern on his chest, watching his breathing change. "Besides," she murmured demurely, "now there'll be another christening. Somebody has to stand up with us."

He stayed her wandering hand. "I suppose so." He looked down at her relaxed body wonderingly. "It must be the water," he decided. And then he ruined it all by grinning so smugly that she burst out laughing.

"Twice," he chuckled, his eyes full of masculine appreciation. "Damn, I'm good!"

"Are you really?" she whispered, lifting up to put her mouth softly to his. "Prove it."

His breath was coming roughly now as his hands smoothed over her taut breasts, over the hips that cradled his child. "My pleasure," he breathed. His mouth parted, biting warmly at her lips, arousing her madly. "What a pity," he whispered, "that you got rid of all your maternity things."

"But I didn't," she grinned, and laughed at his stunned expression.

"You kept them?"

"Well, you might not have expected this, but I did," she told him. "I believe lightning can strike twice."

His face radiated love and laughter. "Do you? Then I guess I can believe in angels. I certainly married one," he whispered against her warm, soft mouth. "You, and two babies. That's heaven on earth to me, all right."

She laughed under her breath and curled up against him as his mouth made slow, sensuous love to hers. Before the feeling burst through her thoughts, she was picking out names. Boys' names . . .

If you're ready for a more sensual, more
provocative reading experience...

We'll send you
4 Silhouette Desire novels
FREE
and without obligation

Then, we'll send you six more Silhouette Desire® novels to preview every month for 15 days with absolutely no obligation!

When you decide to keep them, you pay just $1.95 each
($2.25 each in Canada) *with never any additional charges!*

And that's not all. You get FREE home delivery of all books as
soon as they are published and a FREE subscription to the Silhouette Books Newsletter as long as you remain a member. Each
issue is filled with news on upcoming titles, interviews with
your favorite authors, even their favorite recipes.

Silhouette Desire novels are not for everyone. They are written especially for the woman who wants a more satisfying, more
deeply involving reading experience. Silhouette Desire novels
take you *beyond* the others.

If you're ready for that kind of experience, fill out and return
the coupon today!

Silhouette ♥ Desire®

Silhouette Books, 120 Brighton Rd., P.O. Box 5084, Clifton, NJ 07015-5084

**Clip and mail to: Silhouette Books,
120 Brighton Road, P.O. Box 5084, Clifton, NJ 07015-5084**

YES. Please send me 4 FREE Silhouette Desire novels. Unless you hear from me
after I receive them, send me 6 new Silhouette Desire novels to preview each
month as soon as they are published. I understand you will bill me just $1.95
each, a total of $11.70 (in Canada, $2.25 each, a total of $13.50)—with no
additional shipping, handling, or other charges of any kind. There is no minimum number of books that I must buy, and I can cancel at any time. The first 4
books are mine to keep.   **BD18R6**

_____
Name   (please print)

_____
Address   Apt. #

_____
City   State/Prov.   Zip/Postal Code

* In Canada, mail to: Silhouette Canadian Book Club, 320 Steelcase Rd., E.,
Markham, Ontario, L3R 2M1, Canada
Terms and prices subject to change.
SILHOUETTE DESIRE is a service mark and registered trademark.   **D-SUB-1**

 Silhouette Desire

COMING NEXT MONTH

TREASURE HUNT—Maura Seger
When Lucas and Emily dove for sunken diamonds, the modern-day pirates after them weren't the only danger. They recovered the treasure, but they lost their hearts—to each other.

THE MYTH AND THE MAGIC—Christine Flynn
Combining Stephanie's impulsiveness and Adam's scientific logic meant nothing but trouble. Mythical beast or archaeological abnormality—could the fossil they found lead to the magic of love?

LOVE UNDERCOVER—Sandra Kleinschmit
After reporter Brittany Daniels and detective Gabe Spencer got used to the idea that they needed one another to crack a case, they soon discovered that work and play needn't be mutually exclusive.

DESTINY'S DAUGHTER—Elaine Camp
Years before, Banner's mother had deserted her family for the love of another man. Yuri was that man's son. Could they let the past they couldn't control destroy their chance for a future?

MOMENT OF TRUTH—Suzanne Simms
Michael just couldn't get Alexa out of his mind. Her flamboyance wreaked havoc with his stuffy pin-striped orthodoxy, but when they kissed they had to face the facts: this was love.

SERENDIPITY SAMANTHA—Jo Ann Algermissen
She was an inventor, and nothing could distract her from her work until she met Jack Martin, and a flash of genius became a flash of desire.

AVAILABLE NOW:

LOVEPLAY
Diana Palmer

FIRESTORM
Doreen Owens Malek

JULIET
Ashley Summers

SECRET LOVE
Nancy John

FOOLISH PLEASURE
Jennifer Greene

TEXAS GOLD
Joan Hohl